2459

Kelsey Minick

ISBN:
ISBN-13:

DEDICATION

Lovely Starlings.

CONTENTS

ACKNOWLEDGMENTS

Thank you from the bottom of my heart to my family, Ruth, and closest friends for having to listen to me talk about this novel nonstop. I do hope you enjoy it in the end.

Prologue

"Never judge a book by its cover. A perfect saying every man should live by. Good can beg on your front door and you won't bat an eye. Or, evil can stare you right in the face and you'd never even see it coming." Alec Luca's eyes were lifeless, cold slates that stared out the dust filled, grim stained window.

Dead leaves swirled alive and down the Cliffside onto the barren road below. An old woman walked by with heavy bales of hay for the quick coming winter hoisted on frail shoulders.

"Mother Russia shows no mercy to the poor it seems." Lexie said. Beads of sweat staggered along his brow.

Luca was an unpredictable man. A tiger, ready to strike anyone, even his followers whenever deemed fit.

"She will not live to see that winter."

“Why is that sir?”

“She saw us.”

Lexie knew this and knew it well. Everyone is threatened the same way walking into the decrepit building. Melting candles for walls on the outside, terrifyingly futuristic below the floorboards.

Luca turned, hands planted behind his back . Soot littered the pristine white coat he wore before dirtying the one the scientist wore on the shoulder. Luca always had sunken features. Lines deeply engraved along the eyes, branching out like the willow tree if she was stripped of her leaves. While his skin was a dead man's pale; his smile lead on a child's nightmares, a thin, red ribbon with sharp opals stretched to a joker's smirk.

“Let’s check on the children, old man.”

Upon entering the door, you are welcomed by a quaint sight. Small bookshelves held many books of anatomy and science. Wooden chairs are seated neat and orderly around many small tables. A small room in a supposed two room home. A living space and a bathroom. Would anyone suspect a thing out of a home so ordinary?

Not all books are words on a page. Every story does not need to be told. Keep them hidden behind their leather binding to become a skeleton of what could have been; to rot away into nothing. Stitch the lips so the words can never be spoken. Hide away.

Alec Luca while a smart man, an IQ ascending above Einstein's brilliance, manners of a gentleman; was a psychotic monster who had every last drop of knowledge to this fact. Anastas Mikoyan, a Bolshevik and Soviet statesman did not know of Luca's intentions when he hired him. A poor mistake the world just could not afford to of been made.

Click.

A pristine novel clattered to Lexie's boot and the quaint little bookshelf groaned alive, turning its hinges on their own last leg. The darkness before the men, glow to life with fluorescent beams guiding down winding, steel stairs.

Alec turned to Lexie whose face was scrunched momentarily at the displeasure of the doctor's boots shriek. The older man merely smiled, as if to not take notice at his discomfort. Alec was an extravagant man, there was no doubt. Elaborate galas each evening at his gilded mansion that rested herself upon a hill overlooking Moscow. The fine wines, the lovely ladies who were always fawning and draping their cloaks and selves upon him. The money was never sparse at hand; always enough to shower useless people who will die mortal with useless gifts. Alec Luca was a man many wished they could be. Wish to know at such parties. Or kill to become another Mr. Luca.

A glowing light.

It is what many who have stared death in the face and spat in her eyes claim to see. The men walked towards it and when Lexie's retinas blinked alive to adjust, he saw it all in the medical horror.

The doors hummed to life with a hiss as they parted. Glossy white floors clicked and clicked with the echoes of the doctors walking along them in rapid pace. Opal lights were the glow the man had seen before hand, humming as they dimmed in and out of life. How could any scientist work with such unstable lights? Keys were punched in haste to gather as much data as possible by men and women alike. None of this had frightened Lexie. It was a part of any

Clerk manship he could find a few towns over from the cabin in the wood.

The mason jars were a sight.

“Come, old man. Jon says she is ready.”

She was beautiful indeed, but alive was the true astonishment. For in the jar, floating amidst the blazing jade solution was 0101. A small, royal blue embryo with a dragon's spiked tail floated around at a microscopic level.

Of all the failures, of all the exploded carcasses of orphans and women, whose only purpose was to please the lowly bar tend. This being alive and thriving, born out of pure formulated science.

“Who would have had the audacious thought that what begins human life, but is not human itself, would be that final ingredient we so stupidly overlooked?” Lexie had forgotten the doctors haunting presence.

Now seeing this life form for what it was, he realized he had no thought on what it truly was. For human it was not. Normal was an illusion to its growing mind.

“She’s already adjusting quite well sir. Her tissue levels have begun to bond with the beta radiation and Ph to the nuclear liquids.” A scientist informed the two whilst writing in scribbles along a pad the data he is receiving every minute. The haunting glowing neon cast itself on his face and sent a flash of light across his glass; glinting along the jars.

“Yes, but what is she? Do you even know what it is that you have created? “Lexie could feel the bile rising in his esophagus.

Whatever the embryo was floating around in, born and forever attached to, will have its consequence. But, who will be the one to suffer?

“That is none of your concern Lexie. Jon, have the blood packets A be prepared for transaction. She will be shipped out tonight." It was this that brought the light into Lexie's eyes about Doctor Alec Luca.

"You're a mad man Alec! Can you not see by placing her within a woman could bring about death, medical suspicion or even the child not surviving the 9 month development period?"

Each word growing more frantic as he rounded the table to approach the mystery man who only watched him with easy eyes and unreadable expression along the face.

The child cannot leave the facility. This was never a part of the plan.

"And your tongue is getting ahead of your better judgment, doctor."

"Mikoyan won't stand for this. 0101 is to protect the Mother country. Not destroy the ones below and around her!"

Luca's lifeless eyes shifted. The gecko's eyes move similarly when alerted of a threat. In one swift movement, the man was across the white floors and a cold, strong hand around Lexies neck in a vice grip.

“Mikoyan does not know. He is ignorant to it all as the world will be.” In all the tension drowning the room, Luca was the calm of the sea.

“Who do you work for? Him or me? Cause last time I checked, your money that bought you a porsche and a more than sufficient education for your daughter, did not come from him. “His words as dead as the children surrounding them.

Lexie will admit to no one, but his heart was racing, pounding with such rigor, that he was surprised Luca could not hear. The man was a Dracula of 1977. Ready to sink fangs into Lexie’s throat and bury his truth from the angels who can save the child developing in the radiation right in front of him.

“You don’t have kids, Luca. I do. I am not going to stand by and watch you simply ship out the most dangerous being since Jesus Christ himself to blow up whatever you think is a disgrace to Russia.”

Alec clicked his tongue against teeth, clearly processing all his friend had said and taking it to heart and mind. His skull jutted to one side. Then, the other and his mind was now made up.

Setting Lexie back onto his own two feet, the adder grip loosened to nothing on his neck.

“Then it appears you are of no use to me after all,” The bullet was between two eyes before a grunt could be heard.

Turning to the doctors, Luca noted the room was silent. Grave of once was filled with whirls of machines, printers jutting pages of data and the popping bubbles in the nuclear liquids. A pin drop would be a gong in the room. The doctor smiled at the shocked and tormented souls staring back. They feared for their own lives.

“What are you all staring at? Get back to work.”

The red oozed along the white floor and splashed around a shiny black shoe.

Chapter 1

Red and green lights flicker to life , casting calm warmth along still lashes. Opening her eyes, she sat up and stretched out in the dark room. The sun was peeking through the blinds and birds chirped good morning song to the rolling waves outside. Salty sea air wafted into the air conditioner, giving off that wonderful beach life aesthetic most dream of having through posting on tumblr and Instagram. But in Miami, the aesthetic of those dim neon lights, cool ocean breezes, and Hispanic culture is the day to day life many only fantasize about living through Pinterest boards or Tumblr archives.

“Lolita, ven a comer! el autobús estará aquí pronto!” The teenager chuckled.

Her adoptive mother was the sweetest thing in her sad little world, but her tongue was stern.

She did have to admit, she was running late. The bus really was only about 10 minutes away, but mornings were not the girl's favorite time of day.

Combing fingers through messy curls , Lita sighed to herself. The hair fell abruptly at the middle of her throat and had no definite shape. It annoyed her to death. Hallie wanted them to look more like sisters and a haircut to match seemed like the best idea at the time. Lotion glided along olive skin and moisturizer soothed the ache in her shallow bone structure; bringing it to life once again after a long sleep.

The young girl stared back at her with rooted amber eyes that flickered gold every time the sun hit just right. Sullen and sitting in a wheelchair; she saw herself as not weak, but defenseless and vulnerable; easy to be broke. Hallie was her protector. Despite being younger, she always made sure Lolita was safe, even if she put herself into more dangerous waters. Guess the saying family is not always bound by DNA is true. Tying the strings around her neck, she felt ready to face the day once again.

"Took you long enough, love. I was about to send Hallie to get you." Claudia sighed, scrapping the spatula against the boiling flour.

The oil hisses violently on the pan. The warming sun glistening on cooking pancakes. Her nurse's uniform was muddled and stains of god know what on her sleeve and chest. Lita never mentioned it.

"Yeah, where is Hallie anyway?" She asked instead, biting into a strawberry, the juices bursting alive on her tongue.

"She went out for her run."

"Already? It's so early though."

Claudia merely shrugged at that. Hallie was a runner at soul and in her heart. Other than protecting Lolita from the harsh realities of life and surviving the 8th grade; it was running that was her ultimate end goal in her young life.

The sun was awake now, the beams glowing along her mother's auburn hair as she let water trickle along the already clean plates. Hallie had a passion for running. Claudia was addicted to cleanliness. Not a bad obsession, just not when a speck of dirt could be the breaking point for her.

The back door swung open, clattering against the pots and pans. A small cactus fell from its home and into a basket below. 14 year old Hallie was breathless. The sweat was crisp dew on leaf smooth skin mixing with the water from her water bottle to cool down out there.

“Hola. Sorry I’m a little late. There was an accident out by the beach cove and I wasn’t allowed on the trail.”

Hallie excused herself around the table to collapse her small frame on the nook that leaned against the bay window. Her mother gave a stern look, but didn’t act upon her distaste. She never did with the girls. Instead, she nodded.

“Did you see or hear what happened?”

“Not much, just a few dead animals. I think it was a pack of stray dogs that did it. But of course the cops always have to make a big deal over it, because it happened on a tourist land sight, or whatever." Hallie mumbled as she rested her arm across her eyes, obviously having enough with the world.

"Lita do you have your papers for Rosenstiel? I left them on your desk last night?" Claudia asked her and the teen nodded with a roll of her eyes.

"Yes, it's with my notebook in my bag. I'm gonna go." Without waiting for a response, Lita buckled the seatbelt across her lap and was out the door.

The world was truly alive that day. Dogs chasing after children who rode their bikes along the streets. Palm trees glistening from the fresh rain that occurred the night before, now failing to dry in the humid Miami heat. Couples go swimming in teal water and rolling in the white sand with pina coladas long abandoned there for more conventional things to do deep in the coves.

Lolita always considered herself lucky. She could be in so much worse. The lowly streets where drug lords ruled the asphalt, putting useless rodents like her six feet into the earth. Instead, she had the best education gifted her through Claudia's every paycheck. Her mind was always drowning in the education, but never was quenched that undying thirst for wisdom. Perhaps she was just too young, they say. Lolita never saw the maturity adults have was strictly through age. Like many philosophers, she saw maturity came through what one had experienced and forced that soul to grow up faster than the body.

"Lolita Garcia?" The glossy veil of deep, insightful thought was crushed beneath reality as it set in.

An older woman was staring the girl down, a large yellow bus was parked behind her. How could she of not heard its brutal roar of exhaust and screeching tires?

"Yeah... Sorry I was dozed off." She laughed, faking a modest blush whilst tucking a fly away curl behind her ear.

"It's alright sweetie. Let's get going. Can't have you or the others be late."

Shifting out of her wheelchair and onto the bus seat, she noticed how overcrowded it was. So many people going for strictly marine biology. It was a common goal of profession for Florida kids.

As the wheels began to roll, her gears also started to turn. The blue canvas above erupted into a spur of colors. The imagination trapped in a teenagers brain, who felt it did not belong there; traveled away into a new land filled to the brim with conspiracy and art. The pages of her novel morphed into butterflies. The light casting across royal blues and reds as they flew away in crystal bubbles. Gold flickers through amber eyes as the inaudible noise of a bee's wing hummed loud; louder in her ear. The stars come alive in broad daylight. They glow brighter than their mother and dance around the moon.

How can no one see this beauty? Instead everyone hides away in their phones, their books that drain away the time, or they stare aimlessly and see only a tree. Not a glass lung branching out emerald leaves to give life to all on Mother Earth. Or that in the coming fall season; the trees become stained glass artwork, scattering their colors along the streets when the wind whistles his melodious tune.

Perhaps this particular world is not meant for everyone. Certain masses hold that reputation to burn every beautiful, weird, crazily innocent thing in its path. Leaving a dark and gritty reality in their wake. So, keeping it hidden in the imagination, will forever protect this garden. Just like that, the butterflies became pages once more, the trees stand still, and the stars hide behind the sky. Safe and hidden under the real world.

Others on the bus murmur and they whisper. Every so often glancing at the small girl in the back. Wheels strapped down securely to the floor beside where she sat. The looks they gave did not bother her in the slightest. She was used to the gawking since she was four years old and the children would practically interrogate her.

When she was six years old, Lita vividly recalled the time she was in the hospital. The doctors wanted to cut through her body and twist her intestines around to, in some way, make her life a little bit easier. She remembered sitting by the window. Watching the children run around the garden, being sure to mind the IV's sticking out of their soft skin. She remembered seeing him. Wide brown eyes staring at her in complete awe. The monitors gently hum to life, growing louder as he made his way across the deep blue carpet to her side. The world was moving in slowly, a dream like sequence that was so calm; an eerie aura enveloped itself in the scene. A small hand rested on her wheel. It was not attached to her body, yet she flinched anyway as if he grasped her bicep.

"Why are you in a wheelchair?" The voice was small coming from him. She expected such.

He seemed about 6 years old as she was, but spoke like a toddler.

It irritated her.

Turning her head, she went back to watching the children play. A gloss coating her eyes. Lolita could feel his eyes burning into the back of her skull, but she did not give in. Her stomach was burning from the knife that invaded her body hours ago and the acids danced lively around within. The patience she had was running dangerously thin, even with her family. This boy was not helping.

After what seemed like an eternity, his presence dissipated into nothing. But, it did not last long. She overheard his small voice now contorting to a whine.

“She won’t tell me why, mama”

“Well, go ask her again till she answers ya.”

BANG.

A bundle of black feathers smashed against her window before falling dead to the road. The black exploding in red climbing high into the sky as the rest was mutilated beneath tires. Her heart was a pounding war drum at its climax. She had seen many birds in her life die due to stupidity. Never had an animal ever been so suicidal to of killed itself in such a vulgar way with no remorse or knowledge of the consequence and pain involved.

“Whoa, that was crazy man,” a boy sitting across from her laughed.

His cell phone was tucked away, no doubt that he had just filmed the experience and caught her mortified reaction.

"Yeah. Crazy," she responded before glancing back at the shattered glass.

A single black feather clung to a shard before floating away and disappearing behind the bus. Casting away into oblivion.

The gray and black buildings stacked on top of one another, with the occasional green leaf of a palm tree; at last gave away to palm trees everywhere and long white buildings. ROSENSTIEL SCHOOL OF MARINE & ATMOSPHERIC SCIENCE was in bold along the sides of many buildings the bus rolled by. It stopped beside a dome with a large U in half orange color and the other, a teal side. Chatter of excitement rang among the students and phones flew to social media apps, such as Instagram and Snapchat stories to post this experience. Lolita watched the waves roll in on hot sand and she smiled. The water was her home and the creatures within it marveled her to no possible end.

The bus driver released her wheels from their constraints and allowed Lolita onto the ramp, letting her back down onto the asphalt. The other students were to wrapped up in the science center to really stare or awkwardly shuffle away. Seagulls soared overhead and rested on the branches outstretched to the small structures plotted along the campus. A very calm scene filled with scientific exploration. Lolita couldn't be happier.

Her phone came to life. A notification from her sister appeared.

HALLIE: Have fun at your career center thing. Te quiera! Xoxo.

Lolita smiled and glanced around. She was alone for the students were wandering about as they waited for an official to come out and begin the tour. Her fingers blurred along the electronic screen.

LITA: I love you too, see you tonight.

The doors opened with a hiss. A very futuristic feeling resided in her. When the light and darkness adjusted in her eyes, she saw a woman approach the group.

She was very beautiful. Her dark hair fell just past a sharply framed face, but her smile was warm as the sun basking against it.

"Sorry, I was running a little late. I'm Miss Frazier and I am a professor her at Rosenstiel. Now if you'll follow me we can begin the tour. I think you would like to see the cool stuff first before we go through the classrooms," the scientist leaned ever so slightly towards them, "I'm sure you can already guess how amazing those look."

Miss Frazier turned; the navy blue skirt flowed under a white lab coat as she stepped inside. This woman was confident in what she did and Lolita had to just sit and admire that. One day, she hoped to be that fearless attitude and still have a sweet personality intact.

The inside was just as satisfying, but in different ways. Polished, to where dust was extinct in every nook visible to her eye. Water splashed against a clear case that was held strongly by steel beams. A calm navy light cast itself along the water. The waves rolled in certain patters along its container on an endless cycle within its own.

"Miss Frazier, what exactly is this thing?" A girl by the name of Blair asked, her fingernail gently running along the glass.

The woman turned and pursed her plum glossed lips into a thin line. A stark contrast from their natural luscious state. Walking over to the teen, she bent forward at the waist. This allowed the calm light to cast itself across her soft features.

"Well, it's known as the SUSTAIN. But, in basic human terms; it's just a hurricane simulator. At different pressures and speeds of oxygen, this can simulate just how bad and accurate a hurricane will be given all the other circumstances."

Lolita sat there in the shadows listening to the woman speak and it dawned on her. What was it like to be *that* intelligent? Was the mind like a computer, constantly storing away files until they are needed most? Do they ever overflow? But even though you barely have enough room for the information you already have, you're just starving for more. Yet, no matter how much you consume, never will it be enough. Or, was this brunette's brain like a forest? An endless valley of knowledge that are daisies under a warm sun. Or are they trees, soaring and scraping their branches against the sky, because there is no more room for the knowledge to grow, to expand?

Lita could never ask this woman any of her questions of what it's like to be so smart. She would think she was crazy. She could never ask her those questions, but she could at least know her name.

Her tires were screeching along the polished floors. The sounds were soft door mouse squeals, but rang in her ears; flushing her face to embarrassment. Her fingers placed themselves along the white coat. One she hoped to wear one of these days. Miss Frazier turned with a warm smile across her face.

"Hi, can I help you?"

Her voice was lower than she had expected. But made silk feel like a scrap of sandpaper.

"Well, I just wanted to introduce myself. Seems everyone else already has," she was surprised at how level each word came out, "I'm Lolita."

"Vee."

Her hand extended to the teen and with a slight moment of hesitation, she returned the gesture.

Suddenly, the world contorted in ways nightmares created. Greens and reds splashed about the room and not only did it spin; it jumped twirled and shuddered as if it were cold. She heard voices but, they were alien to her ears. The lights exploded over her head; sending embers of light flying down upon the heads of those around them A blackness began to pool and grow its own pulse in the back of her eyes. The figures of black pulsated like a vein and became outlined in fiery red; growing and growing in her sight. Her world becoming a burnt out piece of film. Consuming ever so slowly until there was nothing left. The world was space. A black vacuum not even sound could penetrate and be heard.

When Vee first saw the girl in the wheelchair, she did not think what everyone else she assumed would when staring through the window. *Poor defenseless girl. Perhaps there was also something wrong-- up there.* The rest of the group rarely acknowledged her presence and it did anger her. Vee never could understand why because someone was different, they automatically were given the outcast label and sent away to the corner.

When she shook this Lolita's hand, she felt a warmth there. A safety blanket tossed along her shoulder. But, the touch grew hot. Hotter--hotter. The blood in her veins ran to ice before stopping all together.

"Miss. Frazier?" She turned to see her partner, Alec Swartz staring at her in bewilderment.

Something was wrong. Badly wrong.

Vee opened her mouth, but no sound came out. One hand gripped her throat while the other held for dear life to the young girl in the wheelchair who seemed to be having the exact same reaction. She made a strange, choking sound; her eyes widened to saucers and she suddenly slid from the weakening grasp. She fell to the floor on her back, the hand holding her throat landed beside her head as the other fell across her stomach.

Lolita had fallen from her wheelchair and landed numbly beside the woman, her face calm and absolute. They never heard the alarms of an invasion ,or their peers being ushered out of the room in a panic and heated frenzy. They didn’t see the glass windows shattering and the doctors on sight shielding their eyes from bright flashing lights and the yells of what sounded like soldiers tongue. They did not see, they did not hear. The mind was shut down.

Chapter 2

When Vee awoke, she was not on the floor in the simulation room like where she remembered shaking Lolita's hand. She was in a bed that felt of soft swan feathers. A monitor was crying beside her in calming beeps. In her hazed vision, she made out an IV on her hand and a black liquid coursing through the tube and into her veins. It was not viscous or thin at all, appearing to make blood or honey out to be thin as water. The lights overhead were blinding over her eyes. A woman was at her side. Beamed from the light it seemed.

"Andrevenya? Can you hear me?" The nurse's voice was soothing.

A calm spring drizzling over her aching and dry mind. Despite the pain behind her cornea, she knew she was not on death row. That was the only positivity. The scientist tried to speak, but the words came out a slur of groans and murmurs followed by sharp hisses of escaping oxygen and carbon dioxide.

"One second love." Vee felt a device be lifted from her cracked lips.

The oxygen mask was held nearby just in case the situation turned dire.

"Vee… I go by Vee."

"Ok. Well Vee, we were quite worried. We nearly lost you and that young lady we found beside you on the scene." This nurse leaned in and cleared in the brunette's glossy vision.

Her auburn hair fell in soft waves along her shoulders. Had a sweet rounded face with calm emeralds staring into her eyes.

Lolita.

"Where is she?"

"She's down the hall. She's alright, don't worry ma'am." The young lady stood upright, again falling back into the blurred vision whilst placing the mask over Vee's mouth.

The cold hand on her right wrist caused the woman to jerk sharply.

“No.”

The nurse’s hands were off the assortment of beaded bracelets guarding soft skin of her wrist, as if she had been burned.

“I just was going to check your pulse dear.”

“Then check the other one.” She had no regret in being sharp with the woman so young she was practically a girl herself.

The nurse did just that and gave one last look at the jewelry lying there. The largest was hand woven, it seemed. With intricate tribal patterns stitched all the way around. Two small earthly toned beaded strings coiled themselves around the woman's small wrist both above and below the large patch of material.

The white room went into an eerie navy blue of darkness and the nurse was gone. Leaving Vee to wonder why she was there to begin with.

“Doctor Brant.” Nurse Kelly called, rushing down the hall. Bypassing the sick children, lining the walls.

Her heart was racing and the mind crawling up this dark hole of questions just praying to whomever was above, that this man had answers.

The man was old. Fine lines along his face each a gained note of wisdom being around unknown sciences waiting like the children to be discovered, analyzed, and treated properly.

“While patients Lolita Garcia and Andrevenya Frazier were unconscious from the trauma aftershock, Nurse Collins and I had removed all jewelry from the bodies to be properly analyzed. We may have discovered something that will require some form of further investigation.” The woman said staring up at her colleague, desperately waiting for a response.

“Kelly, you and I have known each other for years. We don’t need to be so formal,” his words were calm and collect as he smiled tightly. “Just tell me what it is.”

Kelly nodded and exhaled slowly.

“We found imprints on the subject's wrists. Each, on the left.”

“What? Like tattoos?”

“No sir. They appeared to be brandings. A combination of numbers. “She said shakily, “on Andrevenya, it was 0101 and on Lolita; 2459.”

Fear writhed within her core before she licked dulling lips and continued.

“I have reason to believe their blood should be tested, or at least questioned. Sir, what if they were from a form of concentration camp? Or, perhaps worse.”

The doctor looked down, seeing the photographs the nurse had produced from a manila folder. The markings were aged and the skin seemed to pulsate through the ink on the paper.

"No. These brandings weren't from an iron or poker. It seems like it was done beneath the skin and a very long time ago." He said smoothly, but confusion began to boil inside.

"See how the skin is otherwise unbothered around the digits? It means these markings have been there in the body for quite some time. Get me samples of their blood. I want it tested for everything possible."

And with that, Dr. Brant was gone; leaving the young nurse with no answers she craved. Just more questions.

"Are you *sure* you're alright?" Claudia's hands had to be pried from the sides of Lolita's face with a small grunt on the girls part. From there, she held them tight in her palms.

"Yes, I'm sure. The doctors said they will run a few tests before letting me come home."

"What could it possibly of been? Did you eat at all today?"

"Yes mama," the teenager had to chuckle exasperated at this point, "really, I did. Promise."

Lolita eyed Hallie, whom only seemed to be there physically. Mentally, she was elsewhere. Was she in shock that she had almost lost the only person she could call, sister? The lawyers and social workers would embed it into an orphan's brain at such a young age; no matter what family you go to, you will never truly be *their child.* She must of gotten lucky with Hallie and Claudia. They both tried their best, building a safe environment. Wishing for nothing and be given everything. All for one, small detail. Heritage. Common understanding. A family you can call your own and prove it too. Never will she hate this little group of hers. Always will she be in debt. Does Hallie see that too? The gritty reality finally settling in on their fantasy world in the Miami heat, a paradise in itself holding theirs as well?

Two days had passed. The storms were rolling in on black steeds made in the clouds. They grew to a larger army of precipitation and grew blacker and navy blue. The thunder rolled above the towering hospital and small droplets of God's tears dripped onto the window panes. Sobbing down the bricks; staining in their wake. Miami's heat fled the cold, but will return soon. Vee hated the storms. It always grabbed her by the soul and dragged it by the ankles into the dark endless hole of depression.

The door opened suddenly, it brought the woman to inhale sharply as she was brought back to the real world. Dr. Brant was at her side quicker than the shadows scurrying up the walls to listen to what the man had to say, it seemed. The sun hid her face as he parted lips. No words came out but, a folder was placed against her hand on the bedding.

"What's this?" Her voice betrayed her. Raspy and dragging along the words.

Again, nothing. For a moment. Finally the man gained the strength or seemed to snap back like a band.

"We took some blood for testing. These are the documents we received. I'd advise you read those. And read them carefully, Miss Frazier."

Lita had astrapophobia; a fear for storms. That's why she was in a state of dull anger as Claudia had wheeled her out to the hallway to stare out the floor-to-ceiling windows that overlooked the city drowning in the rain. She wanted to be furious and finally shout at her adopted mother for doing something so stupid, like indulge the phobia. But, she was too weak to fight back. Nor did she have the energy of *wanting* to. Every so often, the navy blue sky would flash to life. With veins of fire breaking the canvas apart with a deafening sound of a whip lashing the world. She always flinched and hated herself a little bit more every time. *Toughen up*, she would repeat till her skull burned.

"Where is she?!"

"Miss Frazier please, calm down everything will be alright."

"It is **not** alright, let me see her this is important!"

Lolita just couldn't help but stare at the Latina woman. Her messy locks of hair frayed wildly around her gaunt, yet extremely wild and panicked expressions. The poor nurse as well. Trying her best to be calm and not simply sedate this patient only to lock her away in her room until she was released by the doctor. Despite all the tension she saw, it humored the teen.

All humor drained away rapidly as the two made eye contact down the otherwise, nearly empty hallway. Everything moved in slow motion once again. Yet, it was all a blur outside her peripheral vision. It was all focused on the patient staggering her way closer and closer. The wheels on the IV stand creaked and dragged on the carpeting as she inched closer. As she got to personal bubble territory, she seemed to slowed finally. As if trying to mentally prepare herself for what was to come. But, what is exactly was she so anxiously delaying?

"Lolita. Hi-" Vee hated how her voice cracked at that.

Before even getting to the part that will surely choke her throat in nervous anticipation.

Just blurt it out, why are you so afraid? The voice in the back of her spine hissed along the bone.

Her words are nails clawing up and down.

Worried she will reject you as crazy?

She wouldn't be the first to think so.

She will believe me. I have proof.

She will write you off as a lunatic high on her morphine! Just like everyone who came before her. No happy endings for us. Little tortured soul.

Her blood ran cold.

Too terrified now to even utter a sound, the folder was shoved into the young girl's hands with such rigor and force; it made her jerk back.

“Lolita, we found the frozen yogurt machine but the thing was broke. Hi?” Claudia’s upbeat tone melted into suspicion at the strange woman standing inches from her child. “Can I help you?”

“Hi, I’m Vee Frazier. I was-”

“The woman who was found with my kid in the lab. Yeah I remember hearing about you.” This older woman’s harsh tone brought a tingle sensation down her vertebrae and Vee did not like it one bit.

While Lolita opened the folder and began to peer at the contents within, Vee took this quick living chance to drive this adopted mother away from Lolita. To allow her to read with no other influences. After all; Vee did not know this Claudia woman very well, nor did she have much trust in her to let Lolita read this important revelation willingly. Once they were further down the hall; it was time to shed light on the mysterious subject at hand.

“Miss Garcia, I know this will be hard to swallow.” Vee tried her hardest in her sedated state to speak calmly and not stumble over her own words. “ Dr. Brant had taken both our blood to check for any medical history that could've been unknown. You see, I too was adopted- only to come in and out of the system. It sucks to never know your family. I can only imagine your… Daughter feels the same."

Claudia's expression had changed. From bored and irritated; to suspicious and maybe even- worried.

"What is it you're getting at? And he can't just take her blood without my permission!"

God, why was this so hard for her to just say? Especially to this girls only mother.

"Actually, given certain the circumstances; he can. But what they found-"

"You're my sister?"

The women spun around and Vee just could not help the sharp breathe she had been holding for what seemed like decades escape past her lips in utmost relief. Lolita was there, the open folder on her lap and the reports clutched in a weak, but resilient fist. It was trembling. From fatigue or shock, perhaps both.

"Yes," Vee whispered and she could feel the heat radiating from Miss Garcia's eyes that burned holes in the back of her head.

Lolita's eyes no longer seemed to be looking at the women anymore. She was elsewhere. A sister?

Something that was finally *hers.* A piece of her family now falling into her life's puzzle. All her life she prayed to God for someone anyone to step from the shadows and own up to it all. Take her back and protect her from the uncertainty of life without a family on your side in the battle. Was this all a dream? Where she will wake up on that bus from mere days ago and Vee was never even real, but a figure from her imagination? That she was just a butterfly from her books. Or, was it a day dream and she was mindlessly wandering some corridor beside herself. Aimlessly trying to find the purpose for her life once again? Judging by the warmness in the older lady's eyes; those amber orbs that flicked gold across them like her own was what made her realize; she is awake and all her life before this very moment; she had always been asleep.

"Lolita, sweetie give me those papers we are going home and I'm gonna call Mr. Sanchez to sort all of this out." Lolita had moved quickly enough even in her dreamy state to keep the papers close to her heart and away from the prying hands.

Vee could only watch the scene unravel like a black ribbon. Clumsily falling from its spool. This Claudia's world was unwinding and spiraling before her eyes.

"Why would you call the lawyer? To keep her away?" Her small voice cracked against her will as she stared at the woman she always called loving mother.

Now she wasn't so sure.

"Honey, this woman," a glare was shot at Vee who stood there still in shock, "is a con. She's delusional and I just don't want you to get hurt by her false hope! That's all."

She could only sit there with crumpled papers in her fist and a broken heart lying on her ribs as it sobbed in despair. All she knew about this family was an extravagant lie. She fell right into these people's palms and ate greedily the fake love that grew and thrived there. Lolita only hoped with the last of her glass pieces in her rib cage; that Hallie was innocent in this mess. This destroyed chess board and she had lost.

"How could you do this to me? I finally found a member of my family and you want to be like those who first separated us and do the same?!"

"Lolita! Enough of that," the tone was firm with no care in the words that came from her, "did she care for you all your life? She was nowhere in sight." Vee was confused and hurt.

How could this woman speak about her as if she was not just three feet away?

"No one was there for you Lita. No one was going to be there for you! No one cared. Hallie and I are your family and you should be thanking us for even taking you in, when we could of spared the millions we had to put in to keep you alive. The medical supplies, the therapy! Your expenses nearly broke my own back. And now you want to leave us for her? She doesn't even know you like we do."

Claudia smiled in spite of herself, seeing the girls world in her own eyes just fall like the mighty walls of the castle she had built in her fantasy world. Worn out on her eyes like the heart on her wrists. Exposed to the whole world, just waiting for heartbreak to ensue.

"A mother would never try to keep what would make her daughter away from her. A mother would not force her child to never be with her true family. A mother will always do what's best for her child, even if that means giving them up. If you can't see this as a good thing that I finally found what can make me happy and is safe, were you ever a mother to me?" Her words may have been coated in ice, but rang truth and everyone knew it.

The tension thickened in the surround atmosphere and it was getting difficult to breathe. Claudia had turned to Vee, already seeming to of forgotten she was even there.

" I don't know what I had ever done to you, Miss Frazier. And yet you come into our family just to rip it apart!" The adopted mother just could not help herself, but allow a small grin escape and scurry across her fine lips as the young scientist flinched.

She reminded her of a mouse. A meek little creature Claudia could scare just enough without actually harming, to never come after her child ever again. Family or not.

Vee straightened her spine, standing the best since she could remember. This woman was not about to get to see the weakness that dwelled inside of her.Too many have opened the veil and see her vulnerability. This old woman will not be just another one of *those*.

"Actually, Miss Garcia. Maybe it's time you stop pointing a finger at everyone else and take a look in the mirror. Take a good long look and ask yourself this. Why does my daughter want to leave me? What have I done that must of been so *bad*, that she is just leaping all her faith onto her real family?" The blood was boiling to life in her veins as her confidence awoke and rose like the steam to her eyes, clouding all the bad judgment.

"I looked into her file and yours. Public records I might add so you can't put me away for going through private information. Funny how you did nothing when that deadbeat boyfriend of yours repeatedly beat a defenseless child to a wall and plead him innocent in court!" Vee's anger was a monster inside.

Her fingers flinched against her sides and around the metal stand to her left. A tribal drum beat in a solid beat; echoing a hollow sound deep in her core. How could she was a fantastic question she did not know that she wanted an answer to. She could only imagine where the girl's sister must have been at that time. That horrible autumn day. God, she only now could hopelessly wish upon the faint stars high in the sky that she was involved in Lolita's life and could have grabbed the demon and made the bamboo floors run red. This violence was not new in Vee's life, but hadn't been awakened in somewhere near a decade or so.

“Lita, I’m going to have Hallie grab your things before we check out.” She didn’t even dare to look her own child in the eyes.

The deep auburn eyes that flickered gold in thin strings. Olive skin stained with salty water.

“I-- can’t go. Not with you.”

Claudia turned sharply, a whip lashing rush of air that weakly spliced Vee’s skin.

The tension now a taut violin string. Straining and twisting the emotions within all three. Waiting for it to snap and they beg for mercy. Relief from this anguish and find happiness once more with someone- anyone!

Lolita now knew, she was never going to find it with this woman or her daughter. She couldn’t breathe and felt herself drowning in a dry room. Who will grab her hand and pull her back to life?

“Lolita Sofia Garcia; you *will* do as I say.”

"And what makes you so sure?" Lolita asked, not out of anger or defiance; but simply curious.

She could not read her adopted mother's expression for once in her short life. Lolita realized for the first time ever; she truly knew nothing about Claudia's personality, what she was capable of, or her past and whether it was dark or ordinary.

Was it anger that craved her hand shoot out like the deadly vine and coil around her throat.

A cobra to drain away her pathetic life from this world? Was it a settling sadness that was dawning on her like the rising run out the window that casted its true colors of reality in her hazel eyes?

There were no words again. Each second was a millennium to her. Finally, Claudia spoke again with a stumbling tongue.

"I have rightful custody over you. And I won't be giving it up to this woman. You can forget it."

So this was her true color and it was a hideous one.

The shade of jealousy and envy never flattered anyone who wore it around their neck. *But what has Claudia to be jealous of,* Vee though staring into that woman's mangled locks of hair. Family.

The thought that Lolita could have someone in her life that could possibly mean more to her than the one who adopted her, sent her over edge. The jealousy that this could happen and the envy that they now share something claudia never could have. That is what this person was; a sad case of jealousy and envy.

“Then I will fight for her. And I am sure, Miss Frazier; that the courts may look upon me in better favor than the woman who has records of alcohol abuse and allowed a man to continue living under your roof whilst abusing your child all the way to paraplegia. Who knows what he even could have done to your other child. And considering my very favorable paychecks I get every week, perfect home for her living and not one scar on my good name,” The younger Latina stepped into the elder’s personal space, reveling in her overpowerment that was washing in Claudia’s eyes.

“Who do you think the judge will pick?”

The tension was melting fog and the burnt orange climbed up the walls of the hospital. The black clouds had rolled away and the beams of light casted over the sister's eyes. Gold flowed freely among them and smiles on tender lips. Claudia's guard dog inside her was backing down for it had no real backbone and Lolita never felt so free of its chains. Chains she sometimes would forget existed. When she was young, often she was pampered too ignore the bruises and broken bones.

Claudia backed away from Vee, the back of her legs bumped into the young girls wheelchair. The cold metal sending a shiver up her spine. Something foreign to feel in the girl behind her. Dare she turn around, dare she look Lolita in the eyes.

Claudia Garcia left the hospital that day. She informed Andrevenya about the forms that will arrive at the address given to her by Monday and grabbed her 14 year old daughter, Hallie by the hand and they were gone off into the humid world. Lolita watched her go from the bedroom window. She knew she was never going to see her or her sister ever again.

As alive and free as the paralyzed girl felt; she beat her fit against the pillow.

She cried the rest of the day alone in her bed.

Chapter 3

2 weeks later

Lolita always dreamed of a fun luxury lifestyle along the white sand beaches of Miami. Where the spices that danced on the meats sold in the markets cleared her senses instantly and made her mouth water with the suntan lotion that would cost as much as her college tuition, was lazily slathered onto models olive skin before the photo shoot beside the crystal and glittering ocean. Driving by the luxury homes and swaying trees, she knew it was just as beautiful as it was in the movies.

So many questions swished around in her skull, beating up against the sides like hard waves on unforgiving rocks.

How could a girl like Andrevenya, who like her, came from nothing and yet; could afford to live behind these golden gates heaven would sin and steal?

How did she grow up? Was it just as hard as or worse than what she had to endure?

Was Vee happy? Before she came into her life? Did she have her own form of a family? Close friends or maybe someone more?

All those thoughts and burning questions cooled off and floated away into the abyss as the car pulled to a halt in a long white driveway.

The small home was coated in beautiful ivy branching up and along the walls. The windows casted rainbows inside and along the deep oak door that stood proud in front. It was a little dream cottage done in the modern era. Even the garage doors were aged deep planks. In a fast paced world always advancing in technology and the homes always updating in contemporary styles; it was nice to see a house that had culture and life within it.

“Home sweet home. Rick won’t be off work till around 6:30 so we still have time to make some dinner, get you settled in and fill out the last few medical forms.” Vee said sighing and leaning back against her seat.

Who was Rick? That man Vee had mentioned only a few times before?

Lolita did not think the two were serious enough to live together. She unbuckled the belt across her chest and undid the straps holding down her wheelchair before grabbing her bags and placing them on her lap or slinging it along the handlebars behind her on the wheelchairs back. Vee helped with the boxes that weighed nearly as heavy as her sister.

Sister.

That word was still new to her. A fresh new start on a muddled slate. Constantly erased to be written on with a new story and only again to be erased and written over and over. A few broken pieces from heartache and betrayal so many had caused her. But, when she saw the warmth in the teenagers smile and the glitter in glassy eyes, she knew the honesty that blossomed within her was strong and healthy. Resilience was there too, but not as strong. Vee smiled as she helped her sister out of the van and looked at the home before them. An oasis for two lost souls that will stitch one another back together again with a fine thread of trust and a needle of new memories.

The inside was just as gorgeous and yet, comfortable and safe. Despite being one floor, The high ceilings captured every last drop of sunlight and the room was alive with it bouncing off opal walls and to cream wooden slats under her wheels. She heard running water and sure enough down one of the halls was a small teal stone fountain placed within a crisp wall. The water was clear and ran smooth as satin from the pearlescent turquoise rock made wall behind it, supported by a hand carved cherry oak frame. The river stones were constantly damp with the cool water splashing onto them. A peaceful sight and she was nearly lost in it all.

"It is supposed to bring peace. Tranquility even. I wanted to place it out in the garden, but I didn't want the birds to drink from that." Vee said behind her as she set another bag down on a tan leather couch with a tribal throw blanket draped along its plush armrests.

Lolita turned away from the little decor piece in the wall and continued her adventure in her new home. It was a zen paradise with the geometric glass plant holders gracefully hanging from the vaulted ceilings; filled with succulents and herbs. The smell of the fresh dirt brought just enough of the outside world into the home to make it even more of a perfection.

“Do you want to see the garden? I’m sure you can get around alright out there.”

“Yeah, sounds great.”

The sliding doors whispered as they parted from one another and dissipated into the homes walls. Her sister stepped aside and allowed Lolita to take everything in at once. River stones lined the concrete path along small bamboo made seating areas and rock fire pit. The pond was alive and colored in lilies and moss. The waterfall acted as a small playing ground for the baby coy swimming about, chasing one another as young frogs leap from pad to pad above them. The water and oils shimmer on their fat little bodies when they climbed out from the water and basked on a smooth gray rock.

Continuing further along the garden, she noted the high hedges around the yard. High castle walls of mother nature protecting this little slice of Eden within and away from the polluted world. All but one lining she could see. Without waiting for Vee to give her the permission, she moved to go around the bamboo constructed seats and pavilion to see the final wall was not made of leaves and branches; but a high risen wall of stones. The concrete gave away to Acadia and she rolled effortlessly along it to see the vines swaying from the trees overhead, the water bursting from the wall into a pool. Lolita bent forward in her chair, eager to feel her fingers submerged underneath its glass surface. It moved soft yet swift around the outstretched fingers, caressing coolly, eddying in their wake. Its bluish-green hue wavered in her eyes. It was warm and inviting as well.

“Do you know how to swim?” Vee walked up to her sister's line of sight, before lowering to sit on the wooden floor.

Her floral skirt was hiked to her knees as she dipped now bare feet into the pool. Black nail polish on her toe nails shimmered and Lolita smiled to herself. An edgy sister. The more she stayed around Andrevenya, more and more similarities arose.

"I learned when I was about three years old." She chuckled and undid her seat belt.

"I love swimming. Being in the water, I don't have a disability. No wheelchair or broken bones to hold me back. I can be normal, as odd as that sounds."

A hand stopped Vee's frantic movements to catch her sister whom she assumed was falling from the seat, but was just climbing down to sit beside her on the Acadia. Vee exhaled softly before glancing back at the pool.

"It isn't odd at all," she replied.

She never judged people on physical or mental appearance, especially her own family. But she couldn't help it but marvel at the girl's willpower. Her arms were strong. Possibly as strong as her legs would have been and the upper body strength combined. Lolita's olive skin was much like her own, but the section hidden is what caught a wandering eye of hers. The bracelets wrapped securely around her left wrist. Vee shook her head, not willing her anxiety to get the best of her.

Let me enjoy this moment. Please.

And allow the thought that it could be another similarity?

I won't assume it and you won't either.

The sun was no longer gold in the sky. The star was turning to an amber shade as the trees became black painted silhouettes against an indigo canvas. Glancing down at her phone, the bright LED screen showed her how late it had already gotten.

"Rick will be home soon. And we haven't made dinner or even got to the best part!" She announced to Lolita who looked over her tan shoulder to her older sister, a small curious smile danced at her mouth.

"What? The pool wasn't it?"

Vee shook her head no while she stood up.

"No, your bedroom."

Sharing a bedroom all her life, Lolita was used to confined spaces with a cot and few clothes being the most she had to her name. So, as the two made their way down long halls; that is what she expected. A small little room in the back of this marvelous home.

Andrevenya grunted soft in her chest as she set a box stuffed with medical supplies down at her feet by a simple white door.

“Here we are. I hope you like it.”

Lolita moved past her sister and pushed it open. Her heart jumped into her throat.

The bedroom she got to call her very own was the size of her old house and maybe a little more. The far corner was the darkest, save for the wispy white veils that draped from the ceiling. Small royal blue fairy lights were interwoven in the fabric, faintly casting a calm glow on the bed the size for a Queen.

The bed was tucked away in its own little cave in the walls. The lights along the entire ceiling casted the illusion of a starry night sky. There was a TV and gray couches with white fur pillows and blankets neatly set beside it. An assortment of wire fairy lights was manipulated to form the shape of a leafless tree, stood proud beside a clean white desk with a beautiful computer in its center.

A house sized bedroom and it was hers and hers alone. Most girls or boys even would be happy, but not to where tears would well behind the eyes and dare to stain their cheeks. She always had very little to call hers.

“How are you able to afford all of this? Just by being an instructor?”

Vee shook her head, leaning against the door frame with a soft smile. It was deepening in thought. Small lines formed in the corners of her cat like eyes.

“I work there from time to time. Mostly volunteer work and some quick paying jobs around the campus. But it truly pays to be an engineer I guess. Rick is one as well and while this is not *his* home per say, we find it to be our humble abode.” She said.

After a few moments silence, Vee turned and was gone down the hall. Seconds later, Lita heard pots and pans clattering onto a counter. She did love cooking when she got the chance. Taking one last glance at her room over her shoulder; she smiled wider before closing the door behind her with a soft click.

The couch was soft and nearly engulfed her small frame when Lolita plunged herself onto it, back first. Dinner was a success, well; at least it was to the two. Angel hair pasta with shredded sage and butternut squash all mixed in and served with a crisp pink lemonade. The kitchen was mostly cleaned up after their little food fight in the middle of all the cooking and rapid food preparation. Vee was reaching to the higher shelves Lolita could not ever reach to put pans and utensils away till their next adventure. She could taste the meal sitting on the counter wrapped in silver. The steam trapped in its hold, but the smell was stronger than it could bear and filled the open living space quite well. A flat screen TV mounted on the high walls played some show and while she was staring directly at it, Lolita only saw moving pictures. The dialogue and the cinematic orchestra was background noise to her.

A door bell brought her out of the haze and the world seemed to melt from a silent film and back into its loud and beautiful program. She watched Vee wipe her hands hastily on a nearby rag before flying around the corner; there was a soft hum of voices.

Her sister's, the one she was already growing accustom to in just a short time, followed by a much lower tone. It was gruff but, filled with splendor and kindness. Two bodies reappeared from behind the corner and into the bright kitchen. Andrevenya's face was a full blooming smile.

"Lita, I want you to meet Rick."

Rick was a model man. His chestnut hair must of been groomed and set into place earlier in the day, but now was ruffled and some fell in front of sharp cobalt eyes. She could only assume the messy locks were her sister's fingers doing. The beard was prominent but, not overbearing and fit his structured jaw perfectly. Her eyes faltered down from there to the clothes he wore. Very simple and yet, stylish for an engineer. He was high paying and he dressed the part.

"Lita? Wow that's really a pretty name." His voice, now that she could hear it clear as the day; was a welcome.

He crossed the threshold and grasped her hand in his, giving it a single firm shake before releasing. His smile never left his gorgeous face. Vee really was very lucky to have this Rick. She was glad her sister was with him and she hardly even spoke a word.

“It’s very nice to meet you. We made dinner and were waiting for you.” Lolita said, already transferring to her wheelchair and snapping the belt in place at her lap.

He turned to his girlfriend who was already hard at work tossing foil away and placing the dishes at the table that sat in the bay window area. It was surrounded by clean glass that seemed to melt right into the garden.

“Well, I’m starving.” He smiled down at her before removing his coat and slightly jogging over to the food.

The dinner was wonderful and like a dream. In Fact; the whole day just seemed like one big fantasy you have when under a surgeon's hand. Your mind so desperately clinging to these characters it has created. All of them perfect and flawless in every way, that when you wake up in a cold lonely room with only your shadow there to watch you weep for the loss of a family that never was.

But, this fantasy was her reality. And she had awoken from a nightmare. The cold and empty life she had lived with a family so static in their emotions and engulfed in their own lives; that when it got around to her, the time they spent was brief and so forced. Rick told embarrassing stories about how when he took Vee on their second date, for the first one was a love story in a far away novel brought to life.

"Wait," Lolita chuckled, nearly choking on a half eaten cube of squash, " I want to hear the very first time you two ever met."

The adults exchanged a small look. Unreadable to Lita, but Vee broke into a tender smile before turning to her sister.

"Well, it was around 6 months ago and he wanted us to meet down by the Harbor. I still remember I was in a little black satin number and how much I hated that my hair did not want to stay in the bun since I had left it curly. There were lanterns strewn about the light posts that shone on the water surface and I remember just staring at my reflection. Begging it to just scream at me if I was making a big mistake” She chuckled with a shake of her head before continuing the story.

“I was so nervous! What if he didn’t like me when we finally met? What if I was not everything my friends had built me up to be in his eyes? That’s how we met. A couple of our friends hooked us up and when I finally saw him amidst the crowd, I knew I wasn’t going to let that one slip. The rest is history, I guess.”

The story was brief, and yet gave Lolita just enough insight on her sister's life and how she had been forced to live it before she could truly make it her own. Rick had made a comment on how the plates were clean and set himself to clearing the table.

“You two go have fun while I finish up here.” He said, his lips grazing the soft ones belonging to his girlfriend.

In the master bedroom, Vee sat at the foot of the King sized bed as her sister lay on her back in the middle. Her red painted fingernails were a blur on the phone screen. Her chest rose and fell at heavy, uneven paces. Rightfully so after an intense wrestling match. Vee knew to never assume one with only half a bodily function was the weaker in the challenges faced. Her body slinked forward; outstretched like a cat after a nice sun bathe. When her stomach hit the soft duvet, her body slid to meet her little sisters before resting her forehead against her shoulder.

Lolita is only hardly muscle despite the petite ones in her arms, mostly skin and bone, she thought to herself.

It was true. The girl was not just slim; she was borderline dangerously small and Vee could only pray her italian cooking magic could help the child gain some meat to her bones.

Lolita set her phone on her stomach with a soft *plop.* Turning, she caught a whiff of the deep amber locks brushing against her shoulder and neck for the face was buried against the mattress. It reminded her of crisp apples and the vanilla scent from her skin drifted to join it in harmony. Vee was physically small. Much like the perfect Victorian doll in a shop window where only one of its kind was ever created in some far off land and she was baffled that she only had Rick. That there were no swarms of men and women after her no matter where she went with such beauty.

Their parents must really of had the best genetics and gave them all to the first born. As if telepathically, the sof hair shifted away to reveal her older siblings eyes staring back into her own. She said nothing, but her lips parted into a small smile. A tired one from the long day and last few weeks they had shared.

"Any recent word from Claudia?" Vee asked as she moved to sit upright.

That name left an acidic taste in her mouth. Ever since the courts ruled in favor of Rick and Vee, Claudia had shown her nothing but cruelty. Even to Lolita; the child she raised and had previously vowed to love and protect no matter what. Seemed to be that after custody and paychecks were stopped; the love was suddenly out of supply.

Lolita simply shook her head no before taking Vee's place, her head now rested on the dark haired woman's lap. The phone long abandoned beside her hip bone and smashed between the pillows there. She was never one to cry in front of people especially those who at times looked up to her. Whether that be for dependence or admiration. Her adopted mother had burned anything she had left in the bungalow she once called home after that eventful hospital visit and stay. For a woman nearly fifty-seven years old feeling that undying need and urge to stoop to an upset teenage girls mentality after a petty breakup was pathetic, safe for a crude word. All she had were the clothes she arrived in the ER with, her phone, wheelchair and any medical supplies she had in her school back slung across the back of it. She was so grateful that the medical supply company was so gracious and understanding through the transition period from everything being sent to Vee's home permanently and going to other insurances. The whole ordeal was a hurricane and finally, she was sure they were smooth sailing and not just in the eye.

Vee watched as Lolita's eyes fluttered shut. Not asleep, just thinking. Another similarity to add to the continuously growing list she had been making. Drifting into the deepest parts of the mind whether for a philosophical reason or just a dway dream to escape reality; Vee knew how it felt for she did it all the time.

The door opened slowly and she turned. Rick was there holding two glasses of white wine for the two. Lolita woke up silently before sitting up. Eyeing the glasses in his hands and his shy steps into the room, gave her all the knowledge she needed to know. Her stay had come to an end for the night.

“Well, it’s getting late. I’m gonna head on to bed before school tomorrow.” She said already swinging her limp leg onto the footplate.

“Oh yeah, new school. Nervous?” Rick asked as he set the alcohol down and climbing onto the bed, taking her spot that was still warm from the little body heat her body could produce.

“Please, I have worst fears failing AP Language and Composition.” She snorted and tucked a flyaway strand behind her ear.

The sisters hugged and they hugged tightly. Both for the same reason; they never wanted to let go ever again. Not after 17 years of separation and the dread of the big empty world with no comfort whatsoever. But, they parted anyway; for now, there will always be a tomorrow.

Lolita turned and left the master bedroom, closing the door behind her until she heard the confirmed click. She had plenty to keep her busy. Clothes to pick out from her recent shopping excursion and all the makeup she had now had to be organized onto the shelves. Easily, she would be occupied for a good four hours alone with putting medical supplies and beauty items away before setting the alarm for seven in the morning.

“She’s sweet.” Rick said loud enough for Vee to hear from the en suite as he threw back the sheets and sitting down on the soft mattress.

“Yea she is.” Vee was preoccupied with removing her eye makeup from the day.

Her day outfit that consisted of a navy blue blouse and jeans with red wedges were swapped out for one of her boyfriend's oversized graphic tee shirts and thin thigh high black socks. Her legs were always cold no matter how many blankets she swaddled them in. Especially living in humid Miami; her frigid limbs always confused her. But, her boyfriend always told her how “ *sexy*” her night look was, so it didn’t bother her too much. Setting the brush down, she watched the straight locks form a frizzy curl as the products loosened their strong hold.

When she had stared at her naked face long enough in the mirror, she shut off the light and padded across the fur rug. Her footfalls were feathers on the fabric, before making a fall effortless onto the man splayed out before her. Her face buried into his chest, she inhaled his scent. The sweet citrus was perfectly blended with jasmine and soft flicks of burning wood from a log cabin deep in the snowy mountains.

He was not a Miami native and she knew all the cologne in the world could not detour from his natural aroma that she loved so deeply. It made her feel safe and that his arms were those sturdy walls she could hide behind from the harsh storms life threw her way.

"Hey, you alright bebe?"

The way his fingers combed through her hair and gave those slight pulls sent ticklish electric jolts down her scalp to her spine. His other hand roamed down the column of her spine to rub small circled through the thin white fabric. She could only nod against him with a soft sound of approval. She looked up at him before sitting up to straddle his chest; already regretting the loss of contact she had just then.

“ I just never thought I’d have more of a family, outside of you.” She chuckled.

The expression of confusion mixed with that angelic smile just turned her heart to liquid and drip down her body. She leaned forward and rested her delicate finger tips at both sides of his jaw to trace ever so gently. He leaned up and caught her parted lips in an unexpected kiss. A shudder ran down her muscles and a gasp swallowed by his eager mouth. They parted when air was needed and she stared deep into those oceans. They were dark with desire and it made her wonder why tonight was one different than the others.

“I should be asking you what's up.” She whispered leaning down till her chest pressed against his own.

The warm way he tensed his stomach before relaxing made her smile. His fingers weaved their way through the brunette's short hair at the nape.

"I just always wanted a family with you. And I couldn't be happier that Lita is in our lives. You are so lucky you found her, you know. Many siblings or even sons and daughters never see one another in their lifetime. "

His hand caressed her cheek and she was putty in it. Her face pressing harder against it, kissing the pad of his thumb when it got close enough. Rick did things she could not explain to her. She knew one day he was going to pop that question every girl wishes in her princess diary hidden under her pillow would be asked by her very own prince charming.

"Te amo," she whispered and she meant each and every word.

She really did love him with all her heart.

That was enough for him. The very little Spanish his woman knew never ceased to send him over edge. Grabbing her tiny waist, her back hit the mattress; leaving her breathless beneath him as his lips made work on breaking the skin belonging to her neck. Marking her angelic body in beautiful shades of violet and crimson. Each soothed with the soft grit of his tongue sweeping across each inch.

That night they truly celebrated and the foggy bedroom windows had to be opened after it had became unbearable at two in the morning. Rick enjoyed the intense privacy the mini oasis created for the couple. No wandering eyes of nosy neighbors or passing pedestrians.

Turning, he found Vee's back shimmering in the thin layer of sheen under the pale rays belonging to the full moon. Walking over, his finger began to dance along the slick skin. Little cursive *I Love You's* were drawn from the base of her neck, across to her shoulder blades, and down to the small of her back where the bothersome sheets blocked his journey. He made sure to be as light as the cooling night air surrounding them when writing on his lovers back. He wouldn't dare wake his sleeping beauty. After he was sure every inch of her back had again been touched by his fingers in every way he could imagine; Rick was satisfied and went back to his side of the bed and laid down to stare at the ceiling.

He still to this day has no idea why God gave him Vee. He was so undeserving of the dark haired beauty's loyalty, friendship, trust, and body. And by God himself; he would worship her. Every inch of her body and her soul will be worshipped and respected unless she wanted otherwise. Smiling to himself, he began to drift off into an actual sleep for the first time that night. When he felt just on the verge of crashing into the pleasant darkness, he felt the bed shift and sheets move. Thin, yet toned arms drape across his chest and her soft voice echoed in the shell of his ear.

"I love you too."

Chapter 4

Lolita did not know what scared her more; the fact that when she woke up, she had forgotten where she was for a solid two minutes before noticing the sheer white curtains hiding her bed in the hole in the wall. Or, the fact that she for once did not smell Huevo Fritos. She did not realize how much she would miss the greasy smell of a fried egg with scrambled eggs on the side. Her alarm was soft bells twinkling by her ear, before she had shut it off and snatched the clothes from her wheelchair parked perfectly at the foot of the circular bed.

Looking at herself in the mirror lined with soft lights around its border; it highlighted her strong jaw and deep cheekbones. She recalled Vee telling her while the school did not regard much of a dress code; the education was the highest this part of the country. Perfect for a girl built on intellect all her life, it seemed.

The crop top made of pearly white lace and boho lace print along her chest before tying around her thin throat accentuated her deep olive skin that shimmered thanks to the golden body lotion she had applied after her crisp shower in a bathroom that was all her own. While the top was beautiful and fit perfect seeing it was her sister's back in her early college days; the best part of her attire was the long gypsy skirt with flashes of cardinal, forest, and cream colors decked out in paisley and tribal patterns leading down to the handkerchief hem. Her hair messily piled atop her head in a wild arrangement of curls and humidity drenching through each strand. She liked how her lip gloss that she bought the day before at the massive mall made her lips shine like the ocean under the earth's star and her eyes alive with black lashes. Lolita no longer felt like the poor girl in the slums of Miami, hardly able to keep stress off her cramped mind.

Now, she was staring at her healing body. Healing both emotionally and physically; not to mention mentally, she was beginning to finally appreciate what she was staring back at. Grabbing the rings from her table, she placed the little ordinate jewelry onto her fingers and then small gold bracelets on tiny wrists. She felt like a gypsy and could go out into the world, casting enchantments and bringing about peace and life to the dead routines of those dwelling in the city.

The kitchen was bright. The vast windows filled every corner with vivid sunlight and bringing nature inside. Rick was gone, most likely off to work or to get the Tesla charged for the day's events. On the table casted off from the quartz island was a porcelain bowl rimmed with olive green lines and swirling painted vines branching down every so often. It was filled to the brim with a thick strawberry, banana, and hints of orange smoothie. The raspberries piled on top of fresh cut wild strawberries creating the perfect contrast with the bright blueberries nestled in between. As healthy as that was already; dark chocolate shavings were sprinkled on top of it all. Perhaps she could learn to put the fried eggs behind her with everything else in her past. Pulling the chair aside, she pulled herself up and dove her waiting spoon into the meal set before her. Every unique flavor blended on her taste buds in an array of sour and sweet with slight bitter and fresh taste.

A small bag was placed beside her and she looked up to see Vee.

“Lunch for today. It’s nothing really special,” she said already turning to walk back to the kitchen as she began cleaning up the cut up fruits and berries to discard later,” do you like kale salad with grilled chicken?”

“Love it, actually.” Lita laughed as she finished the last of the treat and popped a few diced cucumbers from the small bowl off to the side into her mouth.

Grabbing the water container on the counter, it too filled with the freshest fruit. This time they were peaches and a few little shavings of lemon. Interesting choice. It was evident her elder sister was a hippie outside the laboratory.

“The school is on my way to the center, if you’d like me to drive you?” She hummed as she flipped out her caramel hair from the top of her blouse.

Lolita nodded with a smile. Any chance she could get to spend time with Andrevenya the better her day seemed to get. Vee nodded happily before grabbing the keys from a little wire basket by the door.

She was so happy Vee enjoyed Latin music. Considering the two were Latina; what proper Hispanic in their right mind, living in the heart of Miami, would despise such culturally beautiful melodies and singsong voices so unique and different than what the radio broadcasted and the critics called the best. Whereas, the masses clarified it "mainstream." Lita couldn't help but break into a full blown smile as she watched Vee swing to the beat whilst gripping the steering wheel. Her voice was something to admire as much as the spanish goddess casting her voice to the children in a lullaby under the moonlight casted down onto them. Vee always claimed to never be a singer, but she was good. Really good, and she hoped one day maybe a small audience could witness it too. Now, Lolita knew she couldn't break windows or make dogs howl as their ears gargled blood. She wasn't that bad, but never would let someone hear her sing a tune. She wasn't as alive and vivid as her sister. But, she didn't envy her either. There was no need for everyone has talents and that was including sisters too; they just won't always be the same.

The school was big, for lack of a better word. The tall structure toward to the sky with a futuristic element to it. The teal windows dazzled against the sandy colored stones that stood proud and tall against the waking sky. An entire section of the campus was built of those teal windows, creating an illusion of a strong wave frozen in place by the school. Palm trees swayed in the salty breeze as student's brisked by the car and going inside the large sliding doors.

Lita's heart was pounding as she hugged her sister goodbye. The wheelchair ramp fell ever so slowly from the van. She could just feel the eyes that were staring before quickly walking away as quickly as possible. But it was when the van faded further and further away, not to be seen for around 7 hours; Lita was petrified. At least she had Hallie back when she lived with the Garcia's. She turned and stared at the campus; taking in all her monstrous fear and exhaling nice and slow, before going through those sliding doors. The crisp air hit her face like the breaking waves from the humid outdoors.

The inside matched the district the school rested in: rich and modern. Blanched marble steps lead down into a clean lobby with soft wood floors that melted into the classrooms doors and other hallways that branched off like limbs of a tree. Over her head was a long hallway up on the third floor separated by opal walls and clear glass for students to look down the lobby. Soft cushions sat scattered about the main floor in hues of blue and green. The second floors were open for peers to look over the high risen and solid wooden sidings. As she rolled down the little ramp set off to the side down into the building, a receptionist was gesturing her near the little desk she sat plumply at. Her silver hairs got wilder the close Lita got.

“You’re our new student yes?” This woman did not give her a chance to even speak. For she was already nose deep in the manilla folders piled on top of her desk about ready to crash and burn her day.

Lita hugged the black scarf closer to her body as it draped along her shoulders. She had found it in her bag before she left the house. Vee said it was hers and thought the bright and festive outfit could use a subtle darkening. The little white skull heads with magenta floral headdresses seemed happy as they danced around up and and around, even upside down the black material. She was now glad she had it. It was freezing in the school.

"Ah here you are!" The lady chirped, quite proud of her little achievement. Her dated glasses rested on her mousy nose as she strained to even read the name.

"Lolita Frazier?"

"That's me." Her words clogged with cotton in her throat.

"Well here is your schedule, locker number and its combination. Your sister had already covered the fees so you my dear are all set."

The receptionist annoyed Lita. Too nice for her liking. She turned and the metal of her foot rest rammed against strong jean clad legs. Oh god, just what she needed. To be an embarrassment and have an enemy her first two minutes being in the building. Looking up, she saw the boy she had crashed into. He was tall, tan skin with caramel hair and calm eyes that merely bore into her own. He extended his strong hand for hers.

"Hey, you ok?"

Is she ok? She was ninety percent sure she had bruised both his legs near the ankles and he was asking *her* if she was *okay*?!

"Uh, yeah I'm good. But are you? I kind of ran into you." Her voice shook like a leaf.

The boy shrugged it all off.

"I'll live, really. Jack." He smiled again giving her hand a brief handshake before glancing down at the schedule sitting prompt on her lap.

"Jones, honors biology. He's just down the west hall. Room 316 can't miss it." He said before brushing past her and going down the counseling hall.

So much for making an enemy, she didn't even manage to make a friend. Huffing the fallen strand from her eyes, she went on a new adventure alone; the one that involved finding an elevator before the final bell.

That stupid elevator seemed to of been a mile away. She just made it into the classroom on the other end of the school by the last second of the bells song. Her teacher didn't even show sympathy her way. Just a glare colder than the dry ice she saw in a nearby chemistry room.

The back lab table was vacant of any students, so she made home there and stared out the window when the class begun. Radioactive decay; she knew all of this and passed the pre test and review he had handed out.

No messages from anyone the whole forty-eight minute period. In fact; Lita was utterly alone all four morning courses. Even sat out in the sunny courtyard protected by fancy electric fencing alone for lunch. None of her teachers liked her. She didn't need a degree to tell her that. She passed anything they threw her way and for some reason, these adults just could not handle the fact that a student just might be smarter than them. It annoyed her as she angrily stabbed the kale with no mercy for the fork she held like a dagger. How about these so called advanced teacher, harden the work for the students who require a real challenge?

Hallie hadn't messaged her or reached out in any way, shape, or form since they left that hospital almost a month ago. No check ins to see how she was or if she was even still alive. No, being the best older sister she always tried to be for Hallie, Lita had messaged her seventy-two times and was left on read every single time it would go through.

The end of day had finally come. No homework because she was a a few weeks ahead of the classes she was in after her first day. Waiting for the van to come around, she sighed fixing the bobby pins that failed now to continue holding up her hair. Students filed onto buses one by one and the parking lot grew more and more spare every passing few minutes.

"Hey watch out!"

The girl had no time to react as she turned and saw a blur of leather and army green rush her way closing in fast. Her body acted on its own accord and reached out grabbing whatever solid form her hands could. The tires squealed on the white concrete as she was swung around as if it was a ballroom and she was performing a terrible waltz. One side of her entire chair lifted off the ground before completely separating from her body. It clattered harshly to the ground and she found herself mid air and still holding onto what she assumed was man.

His arms wrapped around her middle as tight as his dizzy form could manage and keep them both upright. When the world slowed down till it stopped all together, she found herself in a graceful dip, her skirts flowing against her limp legs and chest heaving. Her eyes readjusted to stare at the one holding her close. He was handsome. Sandy hair and deep green eyes. He was not too muscular or lanky by any means.

"Hey. Come here often?" God if that wasn't the cheesiest line. It was corny but, cute given the position they were in.

"Uh, yeah kinda." She replied, her throat dry from shock.

There was a small crowd around the two and Lita glanced at the backpack he had long abandoned. Multiple pins of sports stars she didn't know the names to and a football not too far away from it. A jock, perhaps?

"Are you alright? That football was flying right for your head and I didn't mean to knock you out of your chair." Why was it so cute when he began rambling like a fool?

"Hey Nick, she alright?!" Another boy was running towards the couple with pure panic written all over his face.

"Yeah she's all good." He called over his shoulder before glancing back down at her.

She could only manage a feeble nod and a soft giggle in return; He cared about her well being? And Nick; a nice ring to it.

Oh god he doesn't even know my name, she gasped in her brain. *What even is my name?*

"I-I'm Lolita. By the way and thank you for saving me."

"Lolita, that's cute. Can I call you?" Her brow furrowed at that.

"Call me what?"

“Well,” he shrugged with the most adorable smirk on his face, “ I could text you if you’d like.”

Oh that smartass. She liked it.

“ O- oh yeah, I think?

”

Nick’s friend had pulled her wheelchair to its right side up position and Nick hooked one arm under her knees and held her close bridal style. Lita never could blush, but she would make a cherry look baby pink. He placed her down ever so gently; like she was a glass doll and he couldn't bare allowing another scar to cross her delicate skin. The he scrambled to grab her books and phone before handing them back to her with the goofiest of grins. Why was this boy acting so gullible and love sick around her? A paraplegic with no friends and nothing special about her. This sort of thing is only ever heard about in fairytales where the disabled actually gets the prince. It seemed he was actually invested in her and wanted to be around her more.

“I’m Jason by the way,” the friend said giving her a nod of the head.

Lita looked at her surroundings and took into account that the mass of the circle was a bunch of jocks and many still in their sports getup.

"So, you two are on the football team?" She asked dumbly, something she never does.

Be dumb.

"Oh yeah, I'm the captain." Nick said casually as he fetched his bag slinging it across one broad shoulder that the shirt strained against the muscles there.

Now, Lolita did not know much, if anything about sports, but wasn't being captain, like, a big deal? Mustering up all the courage she could manage, she smiled.

"Well after that little act you did, your girlfriend is very lucky to have a man like you, Nick."

There was a growing laughter among the team members and she could feel her anxiety began to grow in the pit of her stomach. The judgmental sides of these people were going to come out and she was just preparing mentally for the backlash and loneliness sure to follow.

"Lolita, I don't have a girlfriend and in fact," he bent down and tucked her loose hair from her ear so his lips could hover near it.

"I was trying to ask you out."

Well that just sent her into a whirlwind of emotions. Part of her was personally offended that she herself, did not catch on right when he had wanted her number to further communicate. Other parts were flat out shocked that a football captain for one, was interested in her and wanted to actually pursue anything at all!

"So, when's the wedding and am I also invited?"

That sudden voice made the teenagers jump in surprise. Lolita whirled herself around to find Vee standing by her car, leaning against it with her arms smug across her chest and her smile no less of knowing what was going on.

"Vee!" The teen gasped in utter shock and combed back her hair as Nick took the hint, stepping back closer to his buddies.

“Lita. Sorry I’m late. But it seems you kept yourself nice and busy.” Vee responded with mock surprise in her smooth voice before pushing herself off the van’s hood and stepping up on the curb.

“Hi, I’m Andrevenya, Lolita’s sister.” She said, extending her hand for Nick to take.\

The boy was equally smooth and casual, brushing off the initial shock and took her hand giving it a firm shake before letting it fall back to her side.

Nick’s friend, the one who had been the most conversational with them since Lolita had met Nick, leaned and his face was in deep skepticism.

“Older or younger?”

Everyone had to turn and just stare. After seeing his pale complexion, mop of reddish brown hair and many comic books spilling from his bag, it was evident he was the more so nerdy boy of the team, but equally respected as any of the others. Until, in this very second.

“....Older.” Vee murmured before turning back to Nick with a smile sweet as sugar.

Nick only smiled back. Not in any malicious way; only kind and understanding to the woman. He brushed past her and whispered lowly to Lolita who in turn, opened her phone and allowed him to type his number into its contacts.

“ Have a good evening ladies.” Nick said with a smile and small wave to Lita before he and the football team made their way to the junior and senior parking lots at the east parking lot.

Lolita smiled as she watched him grow smaller and smaller. She finally made a friend and most likely with the whole team if she plays her cards right with this Nick guy. She turned with her coy smile creeping along her lips. Looking up she was greeted with the motherly expression across Vee’s face. Arms crossed just under her ribs, she exhaled at the teen who only looked confused now.

“You could've gotten seriously hurt, Lita. And you’re lucky the wheelchair is still in fine condition!” Being a mother tasted weird on the woman's mouth. She wasn't sure could do this with a teenager.

That young girl merely rolled her soft brown eyes and got into the van without another word. Her mind was clearly else where and her eyes were already glued to her phone screen searching for this Nick's number he had left there.

As Vee drove down the road, the sun setting and the sky casting magenta streaks above their heads; she really had time to think about what was going on. She was both a sister and a mother now. Considering she didn't know their mother or what kind of woman she was, she could never be as cruel as Claudia had been to Lolita. But when it came to monitoring teenagers and romantic relationships; she was not qualified for that job. She had experienced things she would not wish on her worst enemy. And by God, she would kill a man before she had to hear that her innocent sister had gone through anything remotely similar. Rounding the corner of the intersection. The neon signs casted their light across her worn features. She knew she could never hide from the tragedies and horrible things she had done that lurk in her shadows. And she was just too afraid to ask them to show their faces and stand tall; proud in the horror they wrought and tattooed the horror on her veins. Then have the strength to ask them to dance. It was driving her to insanity, her childhood and even recent years. Paranoia was always calm in the back of her mind from dawn till the dusk. The human mind truly is the most frightening thing of them all.

The car swished along damp roads and the stop lights angrily shouted at her as she slowed to a stop. A semi truck roared right in front of her little van and flipped off the eighteen wheels before crashing in a heap of flames. The furious flames heated her skin despite being a distance away from her. The trees whispered among her little car, warning one another of dangerous approaching forces before going rigid themselves. Shakily, Vee looked in her rearview mirror. Lita was sound asleep in her chair, cheek pressed against the window pane. The phone's screen black and asleep as well in her lap and limp fingers gripped it, steadying it there.

Vee leaned back into the leather and allowed oxygen to fill her shaky lungs. There was no water or oil on the road. Bone dry and yet, the car had been flipped as if Captain America wanted to use it as a javelin. The only possible theory that could cross her mind as she slowly inched the car along the intersection when the light turned green, was the man in that truck was one who was in the deepest gutter and saw no way out. Though, it may of been her depression whispering to her paranoia and not the trees of something far more sinister coming their way.

Slowing her vehicle to an almost stop, she considered getting out. Helping whomever was driving before anything worse could become of the situation.

When she saw the gas dripping from the ripped underside of the truck, the van was gone like the wind. As she saw Lolita sound asleep from her day's events; Vee was glad because her night will be anything but filled with dreams.

Chapter 5

"Hey, get with it

Take it to the limit

Fire up

Feel the heat

Clap your hands to the beat"

The blonde, bouncing girls who all looked alike jumped up and down on the asphalt while the football players warmed up for a quick practice after the final bell had rung for classes. Seriously, all 14 of the cheerleaders looked like carbon copies of one another with the same robotic attitudes and personalities in check.

Lolita leaned against the fencing in the student section, staring down at the scene displayed before her under the hot sun. The AP Language and Composition homework on her lap that was already finished, meant less than dirt to her when she found the one man she had been on the hunt for ever since she left the school building not five minutes ago. Nick had removed his helmet and the water from the bottle he head drizzled down his perfect jaw and she was captivated. Never will she be a love sick puppy dog. But he did fascinate her she couldn't deny that. The lie would be too much for her to pull off, anyway.

He seemed to of been able to spot her out of the crowd made up of about seven and disregarded the coach or any of his training, leapt over the railing with ease and joined her at the top of the cement stairs; knowing full well that those were not her best friend.

"Hey pretty girl." He said with a toothy grin,
"Hey yourself, sweaty. Is practice over yet? Thought we could grab a bite." She smiled, finding herself to grow more and more comfortable with this boy each passing day.

Ever since they had begun feverously texting for a few weeks, she learned so much more about him other than his notable good looks and the fact he played a sport. She found out that he loved photography, his grades were remarkable and that he even was in an AP physics course like herself, just another period.

The two turned when they saw the cheerleaders join the boys on the green grass and the coaches just giving up. Practice must of been over. Some of the members disregarded the short skirts with long legs attached and joined their captain with his now official girlfriend. That title both thrilled and insulted her.

When he had announced it in front of the school at their large lunch table, hell even scooping her out of her chair to engulf her lips in a kiss; she stills can remember the semi confused applause and the roaring from the team around them. Even with the Instagram bios updated to TAKEN and the constant kisses she gained from him any chance he could get throughout the day; he also had insulted her by never even giving her what she would always hint at: a legitimate date! And no, she did not count quick lunches at fast food joints with the rest of the team members a proper date a boyfriend and girlfriend should have.

"Hey Lita," Carlos, the mousy boy she had come to know that day the lovebirds had first met, said.

"Hey Carlos. Nick and I wanted to maybe stop for something to eat, I already texted Vee to let her know. Any suggestions?"

Before the boy or other members pipe in with their own ideas of where to go, Nick had silenced all of it with one quick glance before staring down into deep set eyes.

“Actually, Lolli, I was hoping you could maybe run home and get dressed for something a little better than jeans and top.” Her boyfriend said with glittering eyes.

The little pet name always made her smile. Even in her lowest of moments. Sure she had nicknames such as Lo or Lita. Lolli was never one up for grabs until he came along into her life. It was simple and yet, oh so adorable. She never thought it would be suitable, but he always reassured her that she was, in fact, a smol bean.

“You mean like? A date?” She asked.

“ Well, I mean if you still wanna stop at like, a cafe or something I’d be equally as happy to take you there,” his hands moved to hold hers and pulled them closer to his chest looming over her.

" I just thought maybe you would prefer something a bit more--official."

It was like he was telepathic and could read her inner thoughts. It was sort of creepy, but she was getting her wish. She had no reason or justification to be complaining right now,

"Fancy dinner sounds wonderful. I just need to know where and when I should arrive."

He smiled down at her and kissed each hand before letting them naturally fall back to her wheels before bending down and pecking her cheek.

"Do you know how lucky I am to have you? The place is Morton's Steakhouse. I know how much you love rare steak, so I figured why not? A nice little place just on the boardwalk. Can't miss it." He smiled back at her.

"So maybe around seven then?"

"Sounds great, Lolli." His lips pecked her own and she chuckled.

She had much to do before her… Date. The excitement broiled in her stomach the more she processed it. Saying goodbye briefly to the boys, she hurried off, texting her sister in a hurry.

LOLITA: Hey:) Change of plans!!!

VEE is typing…

VEE: Hey, what's up? No snack after school?

LOLITA; Actually, I have a date with Nick at Morton's Steakhouse and need help getting ready!

I never had been on a proper date before and I thought since you and Rick, I'm sure have been on plenty, you can maybe help me look the part?

VEE is typing…

VEE: Oh! Of course honey! Don't worry, he won't be able to take his eyes off of you. But everything else he has will stay off and away understood?

Lolita could not help but laugh at her sister's constant worry about this boy not being able to keep it together. She merely sent back a heart before making her way to the pick up where Vee was already on her way to come get her. She had much to get done in four hours. And even that was not enough time to get over her nerves, let alone get ready physically.

Fine Chanel perfume that Rick had given Vee last Christmas danced on Lolita's skin, but it can't hide the goosebumps that bubbled there in the hot evening on the boardwalk. It made her shiver in the little black cocktail dress; daring her to give in and hoist the off shoulder straps onto her shoulder blades. But, she fought it. Ladies strolled by clad in the finer things, walking under the fairy lights strung about the wires over their heads. Their prince charmings guiding them through the slow moving crowds. In the simple getup and her basic makeup that consisted of red lips and Smokey eyes all alone leaning against the ordinate railing; she felt anything but on top of this world. The pale crescent moon rested its glimmer on the dark curls piled in the back of her head that Vee had pulled back while Rick sped through the evening traffic minutes earlier. Messy ringlets framed her sharp face to mask the panic that resided there.

What if I am not everything he expected I'd be?

Am I just making a fool of myself?

They say to me, don't be afraid, it's just romance.

I'm terrified.

Amidst the crowd, her heart pounded just anticipating when the time come that she will see Nick standing as a beacon of light. The world morphing into one big stage and spotlight was all on them. Lita just wanted to see him appear like the rabbit hidden in the magician's hat. So time could slow down and the sea of people would seem to naturally part as they met in the middle. A coroner would of declared her dead because this boy's beauty was too much for her to handle just when he ran across the football field drenched in sweat and water. She could only dream how he would look all dressed up. All of it for her.

She can hear him now tell her just how beautiful he saw her in what she considered to be not worthy of even rags. But to him; he would see it as the fine fabric a queen would have her royal gowns created from. The dinner would be nothing less of perfect, but the view of the endless sea with his arm draped along my shoulders will be unforgettable. She just had her first true love kiss and the rainbows were still alive and kicking in her vision.

It would be then in that very moment, that she truly felt like a Queen. The princesses walking behind them can keep their prince charmings. For she knew she found her King.

The time ticking by was torture for the girl as she kep struggling to catch the faces as they passed her in a blur. The blood coursed through her veins less and less as the clock ticked its hand away. Where could he have been? Perhaps she now had the wrong location? Would not be the first time she messed something like this up.

One man caught her eyes and reeled it in as he approached her in brisk pace. She thought he would simply plow her over for his momentum showed no sign of slowing to a stop. But, the shiny black shoes screeched to a halt and the planet stopped. The air held its breath as this older man smiled down at her. He was a good six feet away from her, but all in all terrified the girl to the bone marrow within.

“Who would've thought you would turn out the way you did.” He spoke soft but, it pierced her ears with needles and her spine grew frigid.

“What are you talking about?” She demanded of this strange man if she could even assume that is what he was; now searching for her partner in worry. “Who are you?”

This person just kept that wolfish grin on his thin lips. Hazel eyes were melted into the whites, like a bad oil painting and hidden behind what maybe was once slicked back hair. But, only now draped in front of the inhuman eyes in a black curtain.

“Where are my manners?” His torso bent ever so slightly forward in a mockery of what she could only assume was a bow her way.

“My name is Derek. And you are the infamous Lolita, no? You are quite popular where I'm from.”

“And where is that?” Fear raked in every word and she knew he could practically taste it on the snake tongue she saw occasionally flicker across his pale mouth to reveal sharp canines.

“Now, does that *really* matter? Is that the only important question just burning in that mind of yours?” His tone was light and playful. Anything but what was truly occurring between them.

“I’m sure that should be the least of your worries, pretty girl.”

Nick.

“Where is he?” She asked him, her nails dug deeper into her palms, unsure if she really wanted to hear that answer from this person.

“You won’t be seeing him again. Well, unless you can find his little grave. That is if, of course, they even find a body to bury” His head fell back as an ear bleeding laugh ripped from deep in his throat.

Nick was dead? This man was not serious. He had to be a fraud. *But, why would he need to lie to you? You don’t even know him.*

"Ok, doll. We need to really get going," his finger jutted her way in a come hither motion as he turned sideways, "come on. Let's go."

She could only think to scoff at this man's audacity!

"Like hell I'm going anywhere with *you*."

Well, that just seemed to make him mad. As his pace picked back up, she backed away, bumping into a few of the people she once admired, now just wanted to notice what was about to happen to her. But, of course they were all to wrapped up in their mink coats and themselves to care and simply stepped away from the panicked jumped up "peasant".

She had nowhere to go and his long skeleton fingers reached out for her, morphing before her eyes into talons as one clutched a material in the length of a necklace or collar. Closer, closer. In her own self pitiful defense, she crossed her arms before her face and squeezed her eyes shut; just waiting now for the inevitable. She felt her blood warm pleasantly and heard a small hum ring low in the back of her brain.

She heard screams. From women, from men, from him worst of all.

She peered through her arms still holding their X. The once powerful demon now writhed on the wooden planks. Deep burning hot scars decorated his white once porcelain skin. Those melting eyes dripped from their position and onto his fevered cheeks as the cries thrashed and erupted from his throat before a jolt of white hot electricity surged up to his Adam's apple, exploding before her eyes.

The man was electrocuted to death. But, how? No stray wires fell from the lanterns and fairy lights that still shone bright as they had always been. His blood sizzled on the boardwalk as it crawled her way. She moved back before melting herself into the panicked crowd that stared at the corpse, many dialing 911.

She was numb.

Finally the tears freed themselves from behind their eyes as she sobbed. Ugly cries not caring that her makeup spidered down her face and the gentle red lips meant for the man she had fallen for, now lie somewhere rotting, smeared as she repeatedly wiped away the salty liquid from her dehydrated cheeks. Rocks flew out from under a speeding drivers car and pelted against her side, tattering the side of her dress, but she felt none of it. Nick was dead and a man who tried to kidnap her was lying on the boardwalk with no eyes or a throat. Was this a terrorist attack result? Was he about to get caught because someone opened their eyes and saw what was to happen so he offed himself before anyone could take him in?

The boardwalk was not far from the house and when the quiet neighborhood came into her view, her sobs only grew louder as she pumped her sore arms faster against the wheels. Blood brewing under thin, callusing skin. Lights snapped on as she passed each house. The cries ringing like the bells of Notre Dame throughout the street.

The house lights were on at home, but that wasn't what made her cries come to an abrupt halt. No. It was the screams coming from inside. An angry lower voice towering over small pleas of a twinkling tone. Rick was mad at Vee? What else could possibly go wrong tonight?!

Lolita opened the door and what she saw was shocking.

Vee was clinging to the island taking heavy breaths as if she hadn't tasted air in quite some time. The entire kitchen behind her was charred from a fire that must have exploded within it. Rick was pacing up and down the soft floors pulling and yanking on his hair. Neither seemed to really notice Lolita in the foyer. And if they did; neither of them seemed to really care.

"Please, Rick-" Vee's voice was pathetically soft. Red rimmed eyes and pale damp cheeks shone under the light,

"No! I don't want to hear an excuse from you. I want answers!" Lita had never heard this type of tone from easy going Rick. It was scary.

"I don't know how it happened! I swear!" She watched Vee try to round the island and join her lover, but he only backed away; like he was afraid.

" You keep trying to tell me you have no clue how you managed to conjure fire- FIRE and explode the kitchen?! God Andrevenya you nearly killed me!"

So the destroyed area was Vee's doing. But how was a great question. Tonight was just filled to the brim with bad surprises, it seemed.

Vee was full on sobbing again, her knees felt like jell-o and she just wanted to collapse; Lita could tell.

"Rick you know I'd never hurt you! And I really don't know how that happened, you've gotta believe me!" She begged, would be on her knees if she knew she would be able to stand back up after.

Rick shook his head, tired and exhausted now.

"No… I don't even know who you are. Hell, is your sister the same way?!" He snapped his head and raised a finger accusingly at Lita.

So he did know she was here. And she would of felt offended at how he degraded her and Vee. But after what happened that she at that time, couldn't explain back at the boardwalk, did not feel Rick to be all in the wrong anymore.

“Please- can’t everyone just calm down.” Lolita’s voice sounded foreign to herself.

“Calm down?! I feel like my insides are being ripped inside OUT!” Her sister screeched at the top of her overused lungs.

“Lita, please move aside.” Rick mumbled rubbing the back of his neck. Lita moved and nudged against something semi soft. She glanced down and her heart also broke. Duffle bags.

And just when she thought she could have it all.

“Please, Rick. Don’t leave us.” She extended her arms to him, but he only backed away as if he had been burned. Eyes wide in purest horror.

At first she was utterly confused, but she looked down at her outstretched palms and saw what spooked him so bad. A teal light was illuminating every vein in her arms up to her wrists. The coiling ligaments appeared more like wires than skin infused vein structures. She lowered her arms and allowed the man to pass her by after grabbing his bags. The only reply the girls got from the man was the slamming door and the soft hum of a Tesla coming to life, moving further and further away from them. Most likely not daring to look back at the house whose insides were in emotional and partially physical shambles.

Vee managed to round the island and close the gap between her younger sister. Taking her trembling hand, the two moved away from the door. It took everything Vee had left to speak as calm and collected as she could.

"I- I have no idea what had come over me, Lita. I felt an extreme heat under my bracelets and when I opened my eyes I saw a ball of intense fire soar from my body and slam into the kitchen… Rick called me a monster." She leaned against the wheelchair and Lolita put on her brakes to help steady them both.

"A man tried to kidnap me. He killed Nick." Vee snapped her head down to Lolita. A face mixed with confusion, fear, and empathic sorrow.

"But, when he tried to come at me, I held up my arms in defense and I felt this soft electrical hum inside of me. I watched him explode and be electrocuted repeatedly from nothing." The words just sounded fictional as she heard them. But, it was all true.

Vee nodded, leaned down and pressed a soft kiss in the curly hair. They had no explanation for one another. What else could they do after losing so much in a matter of an hour or two?

Lolita sat at the table and watched Vee pace much slower than she had been. The initial shock and upset emotions were drained and left the woman a shell of what she stood for. It was a heartbreaking sight.

"I'm going to distress."Vee deadpanned, already walking away from her younger sister sitting near the dining room table who perked up at attention.

"Where are you going?"

"To demolish the living room."

And like that, she was gone around the corner. There was a dead silence in the house before Lolita heard glass shattering and furniture screaming against the hard wood floors as it was moved against its will and flipped around and about. It continued for quite some time before the silence filled the loud void once again.

Finally, Lolita just couldn't take it. She scooted away from the table and made her way into the living room. Or what was left of it. The paintings were on the floor and the chairs tossed across clear to the opposite walls. Trophies stick into the drywall and her sister sat as the broken center piece leaning against an upturned couch. Her knees hiding her face as her shoulders racked withed sobs. Small and self contained. An inner misery Lolita understood too well.

Moving towards the woman, she moved down from her wheelchair and sat on the carpet hip against Vee's. She contemplated her thoughts before resting her head against the shaking shoulders.

"Hey, I have no clue what is happening to us. But- I know things are bound to get better if we find the right people to help us." At first, she didn't even know if Vee had heard or bothered to listen, but she did raise her head and wipe away angry red tears.

"I know.. But, can you please shut up so I can wallow in my own depression and despair?" She begged with a trembling voice.

Lolita shook her head no with the softest of ruined smiles.

"No can do. We both had been forced to suffer alone for all our lives without one another. We are gonna get through this and suffer through it together." She reached over and pried Vee's hands apart before holding one in her own, giving it a firm squeeze.

"No more being alone."

That was enough to drive the older woman over the edge and her body writhed in cries, both out of misery and confusion, with a deep appreciation for the young girl sitting at her side. The two sat there for what seemed to be all night, before a restless sleep over took the girls on that carpet in a destroyed room.

Chapter 6

The sun peeked through half shut curtains that flowed into the open space of the nearly empty home. Vee opened her eyes and felt a wash of drunkenness overcome her mind. If only she was really hungover. It would make the day far more bearable while she was forced to come to realities terms as to what had happened all in one night. The death, heartbreak, and the unexplained power dwelling within her and the teen that slept soundly beside her. Her head resting on Vee's lap.

The phone at her side was lit up, but not one message from Rick. She couldn't tell what hurt worse. The idea that he could not stand by her when these abilities showed their ugly faces, or the fact that he was able to just walk out that door with no hesitation except for when Lolita was in his path to an easy road just lying ahead that door. The anger seemed to morph and grow into a physical heat behind her eyes. It grew so much that the power dwelling and aging there began to ache and burn.

Pop!

Her heart leapt into her throat and up to her brain to say hello as she watched a vase across the room glow a furious shade of crimson, before shattering and sending the shards flying like darts in all different directions. Vee could hear that heartbeat run like a horse on the track as the room seemed to cool off.

"How did you do that?"

The voice, while a soft mouse, made the older brunette flinch and look down to meet curious and sleepy eyes.

"What?"

"Have you ever seen those work lights? They are like a ring light, but they glow red to show off different shadows in the warehouse while the workers do their job? That's what your eyes looked like and then the vase just happened to explode." Lolita asked, taking everything in slowly to analyze as the morning began to develop in her own personal world.

Before Vee could respond, there was a knock on the door. A polite sound that of course bombarded and bounced off the walls creating a deafening echo throughout the empty halls. It was enough to give both ladies a migraine.

“Go to your room and get cleaned up, we will talk after I see who’s here ok?” Vee hummed, helping her sister into her chair.

Lita nodded and rubbed her arms, sore from how she slept and went down the hallway to her bedroom; shutting the door with a soft click. Vee just had to crack a smile. Lolita may have been raised by a deep rooted horrible woman, and yet; always did her best to stay mature and take difficult situations and find a logical way to handle it. They definitely shared that trait. Lita was just better at keeping it consistent.

The constant knocking did nothing to help her groggy state and as she made her way closer to the door, she hollered to it.

“I’m coming!” She sighed, pinching the bridge of her nose and squeezing her eyes shut as she swung the door open, letting the big bright world into her home.

When she opened her eyes and they adjusted to the new surroundings; she saw three people dressed in suits and other more formal attire. Two men and a woman. It made her chuckle in her head for they were standing tallest to shortest perfectly.

“Miss Frazier?” The tall one asked in a deep voice, he held a wallet revealing an F.B.I identification that brought a pit of nervousness deep within her gut.

She leaned against the door frame with parted lips, trying to process the madness that only seemed to continue from the night before.

“Yes, uh can I help you?” She asked them, hating how her voice jumped an octave. Oh if that didn’t make her look obviously nervous, she did not know what else could.

“We would hope so, ma’am. My name is Rogers and my partners; Blaine and detective Carol Olga. We are here on a small investigation due to a crime that had occurred last night approximately around seven-thirty to eight in the evening last night." The tallest man said, storing away his identification with a tight smile. All business.

"Is your sister home with you? We have word she was there as well and we would like to question her as well." The woman, named Carol said, eyeing behind Vee's head and into the home.

The womans piercing blue eyes took in the kitchen and its charred remains. Her tongue clicked before she bore those orbs of blue into amber ones.

"Have a little accident last night and no fire extinguisher?"

Vee spun her head around to see the destroyed section of her home. The numbing pain still residing in her heart before she turned back to the people; plastering a big grin on her lips with a shake of her head.

"Oh, that? No no, I tried to cook something that obviously did not want to come out edible and ruined my kitchen in the process." She laughed it all off to these officers. Or were they detectives? God she was so confused.

“Well,” Vee smiled tighter now as she clapped her hands together once, “it’s been great. But, really we both have no clue what happened last night. It is just as much a mystery to the police as it is to us.”

The three exchanged unreadable glances before the middle man whom she had already forgotten the name of stepped forward. His body was like that of a man who had steroids for his three course meal and every snack in between. Could snap her spine like a chair leg over the back of his knee if he really wanted to. A real Jason Voorhees.

“Oh but, I think you do know Miss Frazier.” He said in a voice to match his body as he stepped closer and looked down at her small form.

He had a good two and a half feet of height on her and a strength she knew she could not compete against. Vee felt like a kitten facing off to a pit bull and she didn’t like it.

"I honestly have no clue what you're talking about-" The words froze at the tip of her tongue when she felt a cool metal press against her hip.

Her eyes faltered down and sure enough there was a gun nestled into her hip bone and soft skin through her thin shirt. Something inside her mind was telling her the whole ordeal didn't seem right. Now it was just taunting her with an I told you so. Looking up and over the woman's head, she did see her neighbors out watering their grass and plants. Her heart began to pump again, but the look this beast gave her gained her full attention once again.

"If you scream, those innocent people will die I can promise you that. And I swear to God I will make you watch every horrible thing done to your sister if you make one sound. Then, maybe I'll have mercy and kill her, then you." He growled inhumanly low as he pressed the gun against her til she grunted in discomfort.

"Now," Rogers said with a sugar sweet smile. It sickened her physically, "just smile and let us in, if you please Miss Frazier."

Andrevenya's eyes jumped at her surroundings. The cars drove by lazily and children screamed as they chased one another on their little bikes going after the ice cream truck. Sprinklers hissed and the clouds ran over her head. So calm and peaceful while a war took place on her front porch.

She smiled at the intruders and stepped aside, her arm gesturing for them to enter her once safe home. They obliged with the fakest of smiles, passing her by one by one. Before she was yanked in by the wrist; her eyes searched to frantically connect with anyone. It did not happen. The door closed hard. They were all alone.

As soon as the door was shut, the barrel of the gun made contact with the back of her head, sending her colliding onto the floor. The world was blurry but, she clung to the side table to try and hoist herself up as the world did cartwheels like her stomach. They demanded for her to *shut up*, so she must have been screaming and quite loud. When she heard the woman say she was going to find the *other one*, an alarm went off in Andrevenya's skull. A nuclear war alarm just blared and rang in her ears.

Standing up fully, she turned to face the beast before her and stared up into his soulless hazel eyes.

“You touch her and swear to God I will kill you.” She warned as nails clawed up and down the inside of her back.

He only scoffed in her face and the back of his hand spliced across her face. Sending her flying halfway across the open area and slamming into the remainder of the kitchen island. She could feel this personal monster roar and moan in her ribs, wanting out to fight. When Vee saw the bedroom door be kicked open and she heard her little sisters petrified screams; she let her body be overcome by something much stronger than herself.

All she saw was red. Her screams that tore themselves from inside her, was not her own and she landed on the man like a tiger; clawing at his chest until she was pulling organs out with her nails. Those weren’t her nails anymore. They were claws like an animal. The scent of his evil blood was enough to blacken her eyes as she continued till her pristine white walls were decorated in his remains and flesh.

Vee heard voices screaming in a language she could not understand and she turned around. Carol had the audacity of holding her sister by the fragile throat and a gun nestled against her soft temple. Rogers held a different kind of pistol. She had never seen anything like it before.

CRACK

The gun went off and Andrevenya screeched demonically. The chains pinned her down to the floor, trapped in the netting. Her claws frantically pawed and tugged, but the bolts held strong to the floor.

Lolita watched as Rogers leaned down and began pulling the excess chains, dragging her sister; reeling her in like some animal as she kicked and fought her hardest. Suddenly; every emotion just emptied from her brain. Leaving her a hollow shell of what she once was.

“Let her go,” the young woman deadpanned. The wave of calmness and peace both frightened and intrigued her.

Her captor merely chuckled in her ear, squeezing until the air supply was cut off.

“And what makes you think I have to listen to whatever you say?” Lolita could hardly understand the woman due to the thick accent.

Otherwise, she did not answer the woman. Her eyes never really focused anywhere, either. She just concentrated her hardest on what she really wanted. The barrel's pressure loosened on her temple and the gun went off.

Carol fell behind her as the blood leaked from her skull and mixed with her brains scattered about on the floor. Lolita wheeled over the organ as it squished beneath the tires.

Rogers held the netting firm, twisting and turning the material in his hand. Lolita watched her sister's chest rise and fall unnaturally. A horror movie live before her eyes. She wanted to be afraid, hide in some room under a bed as the horrific sight embedded itself like a tick in her deepest memory. Andrevenya's once perfect teeth, had turned sharper and only what she could assume by the way it stung the ground when it dripped, was a lethal liquid, was mixed with the blood, was what was dripping from them.

It wasn't her sister anymore; Lolita had no clue who it was trapped in the net that actually seemed to keep her at bay, despite all the strength she clearly displayed.

"Let her go." Lolita demanded again.

Rogers twisted the net hard. The chain links coiled around Andrevenya's small body till it left their marks deep in her skin. And yet, even as her sister writhed in agonizing pain; screaming until her voice dripped in its own blood raw, Lolita remained calm and expressionless.

"I'm going to walk out this front door." He said, pointing slowly at it as he walked closer to the young girl, she could hear the woman's whimpers as her body was drug across the stained floor.

"I am leaving with her," on cue, the net was yanked in his hand, jolting the woman closer to the vile creature, "with you too. Dead or alive. I don't care anymore. Because you. Piss. Me. Off."

Rogers eyes were dark and set solely on the little disabled girl sitting before him. The perfect prey to the cat.

Who was the cat and who was the mouse?

"So be it." She whispered back. Her tone sending jolts of chills up his spine in waves.

She backed away from him and her eyes were warm with the familiar heat behind them. The veins pulsated in perfect harmony to her heart. The breath caught in her throat as they fluttered shut. She could feel everything. Like it was the very first time she had ever lived.

Every mechanical piece in this world and the gears that turned them at every pace to keep it going. Every surge of electricity soaring across the radio waves above her. Every micro, gamma, and radio active wave that flowed through the negative space between her and the end of the earth became visible to her like a grid. Mapping every move and pulse it had as they moved in specific patterns. Hues of long red beams of light melting into yellow, green, ending at violet sparking in long piano like cords.

Her mind began to process it all like a computer chip and when she looked up at the ceiling; the lights began to flicker in time with her blood pressure. She was one with the technology and she begun to feel stronger every second that passed.

Rogers saw this, but not the beauty she had been awakened by and caused tears to flow from her eyes that focused on the lamps and lights. His hand raised, the gun aiming for her heart and fired.

She blinked.

The drywall broke from its mold and clashed against the floor as Andrevenya shielded herself with her arms. Wires of all colors fell from the ceiling. Reds greens and yellows dropped down and snapped in half revealing their living pulses of power. The sparkling bluish white energy flowed from open circuits as they aimed for the man.

His skin peeled away as the wires parted them with the ease a knife would have through the softest butter. The organs exploded inside of him and the bones melted in half when the wires made their way through effortlessly.

Lolita watched as he screamed in terror. The strobe lights that flickered in frenzy from the abuse of its power casted shadows upon her sunken face, red began to splatter across it as a small smile formed on the lips as his parted in the most pathetic form of pleading mercy. Both halves of his body fell upon the woman caught up in the chains. She shrieked in horror. His blood rained down upon her as the live wires smacked against the once white ceiling. The cords fell limp and hung there, dead. The house's power died before moaning back to life a minute later. It took only those sixty seconds for Lolita to of gone from this sadistic monster, to the young teenager seeing the mass murder lying in halves before her and her screams echoed in the silence, save for her sister's soft panicked breaths.

“Vee,” she whispered as her mind gained control and a grasp as to what it saw.

She moved around the pool of blood and had to force the gag back down her dry throat as she shoved the pieces of what remained of that man over and down the hallway with a disgusting, slimy *slap* on the tile. The chains weren't heavy, but they burned her flesh on her palms. She tossed them aside and grunted in surprise as her older sister flung herself along Lolita's shoulders. Clinging to her like a lifeline.

The two stayed there for what seemed like hours. They stayed in the center of the sticky liquid and rotting bodies as the clock ticked by the minutes on the wall buried in the darkness.

“What are we?” Vee whispered in horror.

Chapter 7

It took the sisters about a half hour to gather their thoughts, emotions and come to terms that they almost were kidnapped and had murdered three people in the bloodiest and most horrific form of self defense any court would ever see. It was two hours when the blood and bodies were cleaned up and hidden away. One hour to pack what little they had for easy transport. Fifteen minutes to get in the van and pull further and further away from the perfect oasis.

Fifteen minutes.

Only fifteen minutes to drop their lives and make the run for Brooklyn, New York. Andrevenya had friends up their whom were also doctors and scientists. Her closest comrade was a man who went by the name of Danny.

She had called him back when she was sobbing in her bathroom in the bathtub. The blood swimming down the drain as the cold water danced around her shaking, naked skin. Vee knew she could cry to this man and he would never judge her for it. When she whispered into the phone; *I killed people*. He only asked if she and her new found sister were alright. Never batting a lash to the fact his best friend had ended lives that night. Danny was the type of person who knew his friends would only succumb themselves to horrendous acts such as taking lives, would only be done if there was no other way around it.

She was forever in his debt for letting them stay in an apartment he owned just down the street where he himself lived. All her life she was always told; she would never amount to anything when she grew up. Well, she was a murderer with superpowers she did not want. Did that count to amounting to *anything*? She knew she had to feel powerful. After all, she obtained abilities all science debunked as simple comics. But all she could feel was a pain in her darkening heart.

"You are not weak." Lolita's voice made her jump. Thank god she wore her seatbelt.

She could only see her sister's face when the tired street lamps on the highway rolled on by and casted their orange glow on her worn out face in the passenger seat before drowning back into the night's darkness. Her wheelchair long abandoned behind her in the back.

"What? You can cut people in half AND read minds now?" That came out harsher than she intended, but Lolita only shrugged it off.

"I don't think so. I can just tell by the always growing depression blooming on your face." She whispered back and placed her hand on top of Vee's that clung the steering wheel.

Vee only scoffed and shook her head. Her hand loosened from the wheel and turned to grip the smaller one in hers. She had no idea, no she could never of comprehended that her life was going to result this way. When she was a young teenager, gaining her early credits for marine biology; if someone had told her that she was going to celebrate her fortieth birthday then meet a long lost sister twenty-three years younger and kill a man who had tried to take her to god knows where because she harbored supernatural and extraordinary abilities, she would have had them checked in to the nearest insane asylum.

The signs passed by far too quick for her. The goodbye from the state of Florida passed her rain soaked window and her eyes filled with tears. The happiest she had ever been, was when she spent that time in Florida. The hot sun radiating off the white sand followed by refreshing sea breezes. The pina coladas by resort pools and an italian man draping his arm across her shoulders while a mainstream song blasted from nearby radio stations. Rick, kissing her jaw and holding her close when they danced in the back of the tiki bars by the torches hot light to keep mosquitoes away on those white sand beaches. Surfers catching the navy blue waves under the full moon. Him taking her home and his tongue tasting of Mike's Hard Lemonade and her not really caring. The windows wide open and the air conditioning on full blast with the sheets halfway down the bed could not ease her undying heat. That world was a magical one. The perfect fairytale every woman dreams of as they sit in their little office slaving away for the Big Man. She had it. She lived it. She loved it with all of her heart.

But, it was only a dream. A ten year long dream and she never wanted to wake up. When she turned her head seeing her sister asleep with her jaw hooked against the crook of her arm against the window; she knew why she had to wake up and grow up. Lolita needed her. Sure it was the seventeen year old that killed the two people back in her home, but she knew it was the crazy unnatural side of her that did all of the work. And how long will these double personalities last? Lolita needed a guide all the time and that guide had to be human. Vee was as human as they come.

A small motel's bright lights caught her sleepy eyes. Sleep is what the two really needed. Actual sleep in a soft bed with no invaders, no heartbreakers, no human interaction. Just the back of their eyelids and their rampant imaginations.

She parked the car and got out. The rain had slowed to a slight drizzle. Locking the car with Lolita inside, she hurried into the registration lobby. An older Hispanic woman sat behind the desk, casually reading a magazine that was six year sold and chewing a piece of gum she was sure was around the same age.

"Hi, um… I'd like a room." She said softly.

The old broad peered over her dated glasses that rested comfortably on the bridge of her nose.

"We accept cash, senora." She said nastily. " No credit from rich people like you. Jumping up like you are better than me."

Too tired to fire back a sarcastic remark, she jammed her fist into her pockets, searching for her wallet. She managed and dug out enough money to cover the nights payment. The key was shoved into her waiting palm and she left with no other words to the woman. Not even a thank you because, Vee had just arrived and couldn't wait to get back on the road.

The room was small and looked quaint enough. After laying Lolita on the single bed in the room, brought the bags inside; she locked herself in the bathroom. There, she slid down the shower wall and allowed herself to release all of her emotions in silent cries.

I can't do this!

You have too! For Lita. For god's sake, Vee. Pull yourself together.

I'm not strong enough to do this.

Say that to that thing living inside of you that protected its family.

"Vee?"

The voice in her head was so alive and vivid, it sounded so close and out of herself. She glanced up and saw her sister hugging the door frame. The wheelchair scraping up the siding.

"Is everything ok?" Lolita whispered again.

"Oh, you know what they say. Panicking burns a shit ton of calories." Vee replied shakily rising to her feet.

Lolita only cocked her head to one side, curiosity abundant and clear on her soft features. A stark contrast to the heart and soulless being that she encountered a few hours back.

"Who says that?"

"Me. Right now." Vee said.

After all the horrible things that had happened. After all of the stress that weighed her down deeper into the sea of despair; the slap happy fairy grabbed a hold of her and she did something that sounded foreign to her ears now, she laughed. Even Lolita cracked a smile. It was very beautiful. It mimicked her sisters but a tad wider.

“Alright,” Vee chuckled as the happy high descended within her. “Let’s get you cleaned up before bed. I want s to head out as early as possible. I’ll even put down the seats in the back if you’d like.”

With that, Vee guided Lolita to the bathtub where she ran the water nice and hot, until the steam fogged the singular mirror. She didn’t want to leave her little sister behind. Afraid something may happen and she would not be there to protect her if the second side did not show its face again. She will be reliant.

“Or, you could always teach me to drive!” Lita smiled with mischief written all over her face.

“Yes, please tell me how you plan to drive with only half a functioning body and no hand controls.” Vee fired back with a coy smile as she tugged away the curtain and set the shampoo and conditioner on the siding for Lolita to grab.

Sure, at first that sounded harsh. But, Lolita would often crack self degrading wheelchair jokes similar to that when she would visit her in therapy back in the hospital. She remembered, Lolita was sitting in her wheelchair lifting small weights to gain back any muscle tone she may have lost while bed bound for a few weeks. An old man was standing nearby, discussing with a buddy of his first bout Vee’s body not so quietly. It sickened Vee that men could act that way especially when having two eyes and able to see her helping her paralyzed sister, not trying in any way shape or form to appeal to any wandering eyes. But it was when they began ranting about disabled people taking away the government's money and economy. Obviously they weren’t the best educated.

They went on for a good twenty minutes whilst going between the two topics. Both equally unpleasant to listen too. She didn’t even know why they were down in the therapy section anyway. They didn’t touch one piece of equipment since arriving. The old man blurted out about how he had to park away from the door because all the handicap spaces were taken. But, never once mentioning his reason for needing one.

As he walked past Vee whom was placing the weights back on the tray and grabbing some stretch bands, the gnarled hand slid past her rear and a small gasp of distraught passed her shocked mouth. The disgusting boldness this man. Maybe it was the old age, he thought he could get away with much more than he was allowed.

When she saw out the corner of her peripheral vision he was walking back, she decided to use what he fell for the hardest about her and bent it forward abruptly as she reached to grab bottled water. Sure enough, the shock was just too much and he was down on the floor. Vee couldn't help but smirk coyly as she stepped over his trembling state and back to her sister handing her the water.

"I- I can't feel my legs." The man gasped dramatically as nurses bombarded his way. He was fine, just in shock Vee later found out.

"Oh what a coincidence, I can't either." Lolita chirped with the cutest smile before proceeding to hoist herself by the arms alone into her wheelchair, go to the pull up bars and do a set of 25.

Vee chuckled at that as she stared down at the sink. She heard her sister close the curtain and the water sloshing around her body. Knowing it was safe to move, she walked over and knelt down gathering the dry blood drenched clothes and placed them in a plastic bag. There was no use in keeping them. Those stains won't ever come out.

Lolita slid till her chest was submerged in the steam rising water. It felt amazing to clean away the day physically and emotionally. Running the rag up and down her body, she lathered herself in soft honey and almond milk body wash. The subtle scent easing her tense muscles and other senses. She kept descending until she was laying in the water and staring at the ceiling. Of the entire tacky decor in this room and the motel throughout. A mirror on the ceiling was more so borderline terrifying. Her reflection from afar stared her in the eyes. Once filled with life, energy, and ambition; now lay a mockery in hot water. She hated the sadness that hid there. The fear of what she was becoming. But instead, she let the heat rise to the reflection and allow the fog to hide away the truth lying in the mirror. Let her pretend she is fine. Let her pretend she can be happy again.

The bath water drained quickly as Lolita sat in her chair dressing in an oversized shirt Vee had given her and Lolita managed to find velvet black shorts buried beneath her bags contents. She brushed her teeth as hard as she could and splashed icy water on her face to wake herself up to grasp reality. Flipping off the light, she found Vee curled up in a ball, hugging a pillow and staring numbly at the television screen as a useless game show played on. Lolita wheeled and parked herself beside the bed and flipped herself onto the mattress, luring her sister's attention back on her.

"Hey prune." Vee mumbled and opened her arms wide.

Lolita wasted no time and did not need to be asked twice. She crawled into her sister's warm embrace. They fell back against the mountain of pillows as they both got sucked into the screen once again.

"Did Danny say anything about when we get there?" Lolita asked as she held the blankets up to her chin, not breaking away from the annoying jungle of winning bells and overly dramatic fans screams.

"We are gonna go to a hospital south of Brooklyn to meet a doctor by the name of Grant Hollenbeck. Never met him, but Danny swears on his two cats lives that he is *exactly* what we need. And it's a big deal when he brings his babies into the question." Vee responded tiredly, already sinking into the mattress, just wanting to be swallowed whole by it.

"So, we are going to a hospital you've never heard of to meet a doctor you know nothing about to help us with something we don't even understand? Sounds like a fun weekend." Lolita nodded and turned off the tv before scooting herself down to curl up much like a cat herself into her warm embrace.

It was early in the morning when sleep finally invited herself into their motel room and overcame the siblings. Now finally showing them each mercy. The dreams kept their restlessness at bay and they slept peacefully through the early hours.

Three dollars per gallon? Vee growled in her mind as she paid the hefty check with a distressed anger.

The morning mist was still settling over the valley, hissing on the groggy water in the river and down into the decaying town in West Virginia. She did not know what town, but then again; did she really care? Scrawny dogs chased an old rubber ball down the gravel walkway. Vee sighed running her fingers through her choppy, neck length hair. Her eyes faltered to the small rest stop.

She saw the young woman in the red flannel and sleek black tank top pay for a few Monsters and dried fruit. With her short hair pulled back into a hurried ponytail and minimal makeup gracing her face in a hurry from early in the morning before the sun rose its sleepy head. Their resemblance was so uncanny; that the window seemed like a mirror peering back to her younger self. It made Vee smile as she remembered the few good parts of her teenage years. All she could think now was how glad she was that Lolita's time on the earth was spent better than hers was at the time.

The rusty christmas bells jingled as she pushed the door open with the footrests of her wheelchair. The plastic bag nestled on her black jean clad lap. Her hair falling from the hair tie's hold and leaving messy strands along the framework of her jaw.

"They only had a bottle of water left. Apparently some kids stole all in the packs besides the one." Lolita said with a roll of chocolate eyes.

"Hey, it's fine. I'm sure there will be more at the next stop." Vee replied, keeping the positivity that morning.

Taking the bag from Lita, Vee placed it in the basket that rested between the drivers and passenger seat in the front. Lita hoisted herself into the seat, gripping the overhead hand grip in the car ceiling. Vee set herself to placing the wheelchair in the back before getting in herself.

Back on the highway, Lolita watched as the town began to fade from view. The splintering houses standing shakily over the murky river. It was a flashback to a time before health codes and public safety. A backward town lost in an old time. She never wanted to come back.

The mountains to her left towered above the small van till she could no longer see the top where it ended, supposedly running itself against the gray sky.

Paint It Black, softly sang from the radio stereo and it was a calming lullaby for her as she stared at the tolls that periodically showed up as they left the dark states with the sun rising with their hopes of getting closer to a real bed, a nice cup of burning coffee, and safe home to lock out the world and the awful forming past. The soft melody against the rough guitar strings were in perfect harmony as the clouds chased them but never catching up. The gray sky melted to blue and back to black as the hours spun with the tires below her.

Vee sipped the monster, its energetic flavor sparking a fire on her tongue.

Is caffeine really the best idea? What if this wakes up that monster inside of you?

Who? You?

Perhaps.

Vee smirked and downed another gulp of the energy drink, enjoying its bitter taste all the more.

The sun was beginning to set when she finally saw the sign. The sky was an array of livid colors. Flush Salmon blended with the blue and violet shades before ultimately ending in the pit of the ever stretching hand of onyx black. Reaching its dark hand to grab the sun by her tender throat to choke out the warm light.

WELCOME TO NEW YORK.

NYC NEXT RIGHT

“Hey,” she nudged her sleeping sibling, the smile only growing. “ Lita, wake up.”

“Mmm?” Lolita muttered with squinting eyes.

“Welcome to the big city, sis.” Vee smiled happy to be back.

“Which is a good thing,” Vee continued as she pulled the car over a few lanes.
“I feel like my spine is going to cave in if I sit in this car any longer!” She sighed.

Lolita smirked and undid the already falling out ponytail with a quick shake of the head.
“Coming from someone who has experience with caved-in spinal columns, I can assure you that I’m pretty sure it doesn’t work that way.” That earned a rightful smack from her older sister in the arm.

She scoffed and bent forward, grabbing the water bottle between them and opened it, taking the last of it to her parched throat.

"You know," Vee sighed, ready to change the subject, " With all this crazy stuff happening; I hope we attract like, the C.I.A!"

Lolita choked on the last of the water, eyes boggling out of her skull.

"Are you *actually* insane?!" She coughed, hand on the base of her neck.

"I've never seen someone kick in a door that wasn't me! It would be so exciting." The brunette squealed, clapping her hands momentarily before gripping the wheel again.

Lolita was now convinced, her sister was running on empty.

" Ok," Lolita chuckled, patting her sister's wrist before turning back to the window as she saw the Big Apple come closer and closer, sucking them both in.

"Tell me about the city." Lita whispered, eyes trapped on the bright lights above her as they began to grow and grow the closer they got.

“ Well, it’s basically where I grew up.” Vee whispered as she steered off the route going deeper into the city that never seems to sleep.

“It was an adventure, to say the least. Growing up in the most uncaring foster home; I kind of ran the streets. Alone, usually. No one to call mom. No one to call Dad. Most of the time, I found abandoned subway stations and their trains to be my home for weeks and months at a time. The graffiti taught me more about the world and all the cultures stirring in it than the schools could. The street performers showed me the every running range of human emotion better than the foster parents that came in by the dozens from before I could walk. Running from mad hatters and Alice’s when the sun fell from the sky and casted their friend; the shadows on their allies as I walked home each night.”

The lights flickered across her face, the fun demeanor was dead and only left the memories to rise and tell each of their stories. Lolita was all the more curious.

"I did things I will never be proud of. Things I can't let you hear. I was friends with filthy rats covered in sins and plastic. They would promise me I would be safe. That I'd always have a couch to sleep on. I'd just have to share it with a few of the local stoners and hookers doing their jobs. At the time, I didn't care. A McDonald's burger was a meal, nonetheless and a couch was a solid bed with a roof above it. I had boyfriends I wish were never born, friends I wish I could rewind time like a VHS and burn that one section of the film. But," Vee turned to her sister.

Lolita's eyes were deep pools of curiosity and a thrive to hear more, learn more, know more. Not enthused about the immense darkness in the past; just wanting to understand it.

"I'm not a total useless case. I could be used as an example. To make sure your life never starts going down such a dark path. Because there isn't always light at the end of it."

There was a silence. A long quietness other than the murmur of tires rolling beneath them. It wasn't unwelcomed.

"And this friend of yours… He was a part of it all? I mean-- That part of your life?" Lolita asked, hoping she wasn't treading dangerous waters.

Vee chuckled with a shake of her head. A real smile gracing her.

"No. Danny… He was a, well, kind of like a savior to me. He helped me out of a disaster of a relationship and convinced his parents to get me into a better school he was going to half a day for a career program. A medicine science course, we took it together and even attended the same college."

"Is that where he met Hollenbeck?"

Vee cocked her head to the side, a confused look spread across it.

"Actually, I'm not sure where he knows him from. Guess I'll have to ask."

The rest of the ride went over smoothly. Some quick sightseeing from the passenger window. Vee would occasionally point out little sights and tell her a memory she had from it. And for the most part; they were quite light hearted and quirky even.

“And that frozen yogurt shop was where my friend, Claire, had decided to jump onto my back wanting to I guess have a piggyback ride. We both were on the floor in seconds. And down that road is a laser tag joint. My boyfriend at the time and I decided to go down there one Saturday night. He had pushed me into a dark corner and we made out some. The the idiot shot me and I remember just tackling his sorry as- butt to the floor.” Vee enjoyed how Lolita was entranced with her as the two shared this trip down Vee’s memory lane.

As the car rolled along Brooklyn Bridge, Lita’s phone snapped hundreds of photos. They each turned out aesthetically pleasing. Calm and inviting with a grunge undertone. Open for many stories to be told. It all depended on who saw them.

The world turned to apartment complexes and modern townhouses stacked on top of one another with small squares of green one man could fit into, calling those gardens and backyards. The van pulled to a rest in front of a slew of townhouses. The iron fencing guarded the concrete courtyards under blackened windows. Some lit with warm glowing lights against the night. The trees billowed in the wind; their scarlet leaves flittered among the world. Waltzing with one another before sleeping on the brick. As Vee helped Lolita into her wheelchair, the damp breeze whipped against her cheek. The air was moist and Lolita could feel the slight sheen of icy air rest on her sun kissed skin. She hugged her flannel tighter around her. The victorian lamp posts stood lit up and their eyes seem to follow the newcomer as she wheeled to the iron gates. The material cold against her curled fingers; knuckles a ghostly white. New York City was an alien planet to her. She had no idea the customs; what was considered normal or what was considered unruly here.

A whole other country from fun loving Miami. Men in business suits brisked by her without a care in their self centered world. All work, no play here. No wonder Miami was always known to be a vacation location and NYC was a one day visit. A weekend if you want to get really adventurous.

“Veeve!” Lita turned at the voice.

At the top of the stone stairs waving excited arms was whom she could only assume was this Danny friend. His hair was a wild orange with wide framed glasses. Textbook Nerd out of high school and right into the workforce.

“Hey Danny.” Her sister said as she hoisted the few bags they had, over her shoulder with ease as she walked up to join Lolita by the iron.

“This is Lolita. My sister I was telling you about.”

“Ah! Lolita it’s so nice to meet you,” his nervously wrung hands grabbed hers with such vigor and shook equally as hard.

“Well, come in come in! It’s getting chilly here.” His hands fumbled on the gate lock and it came undone with a rusty click.

The inside did not match its cold brick exterior. The ceiling was designed with warm aging wood matching the floors below it. The living space had a homey and boho vibe. Soft leather couches crowded around a moderate TV. The white kitchen was blended with both natural and industrial design. Two cats Lolita had mistaken for overstuffed pillows prowled and prodded her wheels with fat paws. Reading the collars after searching under endless fluffy fat; she found their names. The orange one matched his owner's hair. His name was Charlie. The mustard cat was named Carol and the names made her snicker. It was a good thing she adored cats and dogs alike.

"Lolita, do you like salad?" He asked rushing to the counter and grabbing clay bowls eagerly watching her face.

"Oh yeah, love it." She smiled helping set her things on one of the many couches with Vee.
"We're starved."

The dinner was the best Lolita had in a long few days. The honey mustard chicken mashed with the avocado, causing a delightful explosion of a certainly unique taste on her taste buds. The salty bacon bits and fresh ground pepper gave the already flavored food an extra kick she didn't realize it needed in the lettuce. It beat monster and junk food with some dried " fruit." She saw Vee devour her second serving. Apparently she shared her thoughts exactly. After that, he did not stop and stuffed the thin women with breadsticks dipped in hot butter and garlic. The it didn't end there. An endless train of meals. Lolita felt like she was going to burst at the seams. But couldn't find it in her to refuse any of it.

It was after the Spanish ice cream; French vanilla ice cream with dark chocolate fudge and frosted flakes coating it, that she crashed on the soft leather with the lullaby of Jeopardy lulling her to sleep with a happy and full stomach.

"Hey," Vee said as she slid out of the window and onto the fire escape. Danny was shook from his thoughts and held the wrist that wasn't clutching a bottle of beer in her hand, to steady her as she landed on the grates.

"I just wanted to thank you, for doing this for me… For us." She exhaled as she leaned against the railing beside him.

The soft breeze weaved its fingers through her soft hair and stung her eyes. He chuckled and wiped his glasses on the soft cotton of his shirt, while she took a drink.

"You would have done the same for me. You're like my own little sister, Vee. You know I'd do anything for you. I'd even hide a body for you… Oh God," he stammered, eyes widening as Vee bowed her head. The hair covered her face from him acting as a shield.

"I'm so sorry, it just slipped! I wasn't even thinking, Vee!"

"It's fine. Really Danny, you don't need to apologize." She smiled as she took another swig before letting it hang from limp fingers over the side.

"Tell me," She said after pausing for a minute to gather herself.

She stared her best friend deep in the eyes before parting her lips again.

"You can instead, tell me about this Grant Hollenbeck guy and just how exactly you know him. Who is he? What exactly does he do, because you were quite vague when we spoke on the phone. Too vague might I add for your best friend!" Her voice rose in speculation and a long lost New York accent began to peel through her each of her words as she stood up straighter with every sentence.

"Hey hey hey, easy there tiger. Can you let me explain before you go at me?" He asked of her while gently holding her outstretched hands, being mindful to set her bottle down in case she decided to either drop it off the railing or over his own head.

" Grant is a doctor who specializes in people to experience similar cases like yours. He works at the Gracen Hospital. Now I don't know the floor. So don't interrogate me in much cause I in fact, know very little. I met him at a few galas for the joint hospital celebrations. Extremely wealthy and generous man. He knows what he is doing ok?"

Vee nodded, her arms falling back to her sides as a shaky breath escaped her.

"I just hope you're right."

"I know I'm right. Now," his hand began to guide her back to the window. It was growing colder by the minute.

"He is at the hospital twenty-four seven. Lives for his work, you could say. So you and Lita are welcome to head down at any time."

Vee nodded, exhaustion winning her over. The two climbed through the window and he tossed out her empty glass.

"I'm gonna just say goodnight to Lita before I call it a night." She mumbled, almost slurring her words.

Danny nodded and made his way back to the kitchen to wash some extra dessert dishes as Vee made her way to her little sister asleep on the couch. Two fat furballs snuggled against her, acting as if they could be some form of guard dog.

Leaning down, Vee pressed a kiss to her soft temple and rested her hand over the bracelets Lita wore to balance herself. When Vee opened her eyes; she saw genetic codes and blips along her vision. Body running damp and cold in dead fear. Looking down; her little sister was doing no better than her. The skin beneath both their jewelry burned in liquid flames and the veins trapped beneath their skin lit up like a Christmas tree. She staggered backward desperately clinging to sanity that was slippery in her mental grasp. The world went black and white as she fell to the floor. Vee could hear her sister's frantic, choked breaths as she tried to grasp what was happening.

In the midst of all of this; Andrevenya heard her friend say, "Or we could go… RIGHT NOW!"

Chapter 8

The world ran like a poor strip of film. Burning in holes every time she opened her eyes. At times she saw Danny, hauling her onto the couch and then there was a calming darkness. The footage would roll again and she was staring at the roof of a car with Lolita lying against her shoulder. Her eyes unable to focus on anything. Constantly fluttering to the back of her head, giving her a ghoulish appearance; or she would shift her eyes all around. Lolita became a blurry image in her vision. A spilled canister of paint on a dark canvas. The sun peeking through the window high above where she lay acted as a lens flare, blinding her til she just had to close her eyes out of the heightening migraine. This feeling was all too familiar for her and she really did not ever want to admit that.

Black consumed her again. A hole burned itself through the curtain and humans hidden behind clean white masks were lurking above her body. A white cluster of tiles were in motion above her with the occasional bright light zooming by. Andrevenya tried to speak, scold the people poking and prodding against her arm with pointed needles. But, an oxygen mask again was the culprit in muffling and muddling her words. She gave up with a nausea swept through her nose and down her quivering neck. Fluids were icy in her blood, rushing and counteracting whatever it was inside her body. A parasite wanting to be free and scurry along the walls. Break out and feast on the pathetic beings experimenting on her as she lay bound to a soft white and blue bed. Even though she was fully clothed, swaddled in heated cotton blankets soft against her surprisingly cold skin; she felt exposed as the day she was born. The patients and their families watched her roll on by to tall silver doors. An elevator. Quite large from what she could see through the metal bars of the rails the doctor clung to. Another bed rolled in, Lolita unconscious laying there. The doctors let her alone and she was glad. A calm little blip went off as the box fell from floor to floor. The red number one passed and they began falling into the negatives. What kind of hospital was this? How far were they headed? Will she stay awake long enough to find out?

Drowsiness, stronger than the last time it made an appearance began to grab her shoulders. Gentle at first that she didn't even notice its presence. Then the grip became forceful. Unyielding and pinning her down. Her body convulsed as she struggled to stay awake. She can't fall asleep now. A doctor noticed her fighting and held up a syringe filled with clear liquid. Something inside her yelled that it was not just saline. As it was injected into her IV and coursed through the little tubes before embedding itself in her system, all she could think before she lost was; She was going to kill Danny.

Andrevenya woke up in a cage. Not a cage made of twisted metal and wires that a dog would be forced to endure its days within its uncomfortable walls. This prison was a cube, a clear one. Where she could see the nearly empty hallway lying just before her. Nurses paced the smooth floors reading reports or chatting to one another. Not even daring to acknowledge the panicking woman only a few feet away.

She had to get free, find Lolita, and get to Danny. She had to wring his neck for trusting this doctor who only placed her in leather straps to the bed as a hostage. How is this helping her in her predicament? She felt like she was in an asylum. A mental ward.

Maybe we are? Danny did say this doctor specialized in special cases like ours.

Yes he did say that. So what?

Perhaps you are *crazy.*

“You need to learn to control your anger, Andrevenya. Before it starts to get to you.”

The voice was soothing, gruff and calm. Vee hated it. Looking away from her restraints, she saw a man with silvery hair and black pools in his eye sockets. It terrified her.

“Dr. Hollenbeck?” She asked, hating how her voice wavered.

“I apologize my introduction had to start out this way. But when your pulse and BP spike to a near one thousand well,” he chuckled, leaning against the foot of the bed.

“It leaves us no choice but to take every safety measure. For both you, the patient. And for the staff.”

“Where’s-”

“Lolita? She's perfectly fine.”

When he saw that the woman didn’t believe him and rightfully so, he made a sound similar to annoyance.

“Take a look for yourself.”

Hollenbeck walked over and moved a thin curtain to her left aside. Behind the glass wall was a room resembling her own. Lolita looked so small in that bed. A small cat in a football field sized bed.

“We don’t have to put her in restraints like yours. Which is surprising. We always thought they would design you two the exact same way. Like carbon copies.” He sighed and let the curtain fall back into place.

“Can you please explain to me what exactly is going on?” She growled, pulling at the straps.

Now she knew what that girl in the exorcism movie felt like being bound to her bed. It wasn’t pleasant to say the least.

“What do you know about your parents?”

Silence.

"Come on, Vee. We are both adults here. And if you answer my questions; I can answer anything you throw my way. But we need some kind of communication on your end." He replied to her stubbornness with casualty and it annoyed her.

"All I ever got from the government on them was that they dropped me off at some foster care system home and left. They assumed since it was the seventies that they were some stoners or something and I was labeled an accidental birth." The story was ashes on her tongue and she despised telling it.

His eyes were soft as they stared right past her own and straight through her spirit within.

"You don't know really anything about them because they never existed." He deadpanned as he leaned forward on the stool he sat on by her bedside.

"What? No that-"

"Impossible? Well it was until May fourteenth in nineteen seventy-seven. I'm going to have my comrade, Daniel Marks explain this all to your sister once she's awake."

Danny.

So Danny knew all of this? But for how long? How long did he know and yet refused to tell her that he always had known she was this mutated freak!

"In Tobolsk, Russia there was a laboratory run by a man named Anastas Mikoyan. He was a Bolshevik Statesman at the time of nineteen seventy-seven. He had appointed the head of this lab to a man named Alec Luca. This operation, as dangerous as it was, was given hefty funds to create a form of a biological weapon that could wipe out ninety percent of our world in world war three if anyone posed a threat to their country. There were one hundred failures. One hundred potential killing machines built from a balance of nuclear liquids and radiation to ship out into the world to do their bidding. You were the one hundred and first."

This was madness. Something out of a science fiction novel. This could not possibly be her life story.

“We are still trying to discover what exactly they used and what formula they invented to put in such dangerous material weaving through every strand of your DNA. The nuclear and radiation is perfectly blended and coded within your tissue and Ph levels. There is no way to remove it from you or Lolita. Without killing you two, of course.”

“But- you need a male and female to create a kid. That’s simple biology.” Vee pointed out, once she found her voice.

“Well, you aren’t wrong. We all thought that. But, the people who made you two, including Mr. Luca found a way to create live embryos made completely out of a synthetic computer coding program. Look, I know you don’t believe me. But your last three visitors of yours; I don’t know about you, but I always found Russian accents to be quite hard to follow.” He said blandly as he shifted to bump the stool against her bed.

The pale blue fluorescent lights hummed above her head in thin tubes. Casting ghoulish shadows across the room. Heightening the suspense and tension in the tiny room.

“What are we?”

“Weapons. Nuclear time bombs that they had planned to detonate wherever and whenever they pleased. With the intense power inside you both being so close together. Well… You would have the capability of vaporizing both north and South America alone. Not to mention evaporating one hundred miles of ocean in a perfect radius.”

Vee couldn’t stare at him as her jaw fell slowly and her head turning away to stare at the shiny floor. Her muddled face stared back at her in utter fear.

“Do you-- want me to continue, Andrevenya?”

“Yes.”

He nodded and ran his fingers along the scruff on his chin, before continuing.

“ The fall out of the nuclear and radiation would in theory bring about the death toll of hundred thousand across the oceans being carried by the sea breezes. You two have the power in destroying nearly ninety percent of our human race, not to even calculate the animal and plant life that would be affected. And your powers; those were mutations from the radiation being so intricately woven in the DNA helix.”

Her head finally rose and her eyes met his.

“Then why keep us alive? If we are so dangerous and can be...Blown up anytime some guy gets a little trigger happy?”

He smiled and rested his hand over her IV, rubbing the skin around the tape.

“Because, those people may think killing innocent people with innocent people is justifiable; I don’t think killing off two sisters who have no idea what is going on is in the best interest of the human race. The program I run is one to strengthen mutants such as yourself. Understand what you have been given and learn to be one with it and not try to fight or hide it. Because it is you and you are it."

He wanted to spare two out of seven billion? This man was truly insane if he was selfish enough to keep them alive and risk them all dying any second now.

"Fine, but we have to make sure they can't just- blow us up." She stated firmly, but was taken aback when he smiled all knowingly.

"I'm glad you said that. Once you two are fully ready; the endgame was to send you to Tobolsk, Russia and go to the now abandoned pathology lab to retrieve the last remaining items inside."

"Why is it abandoned?" She asked, her eyes widening with curiosity about the true place of her…

Birth.

"After they created Lolita, the Russian Federation had ambushed them to halt production. But they had already shipped her out like they had you and lost connections as to where you two ended up.

Apparently they were released or at least have someone out and found you two together."

"Fine, we'll do it. Find whatever it is so they can't use us." She said slowly.

"Great," he smiled standing up and grabbed his notepad. " I will see Daniel briefs Lolita."

As he left, Vee laid her head back down staring at the ceiling with broken eyes.

What has she agreed to?

Chapter 9

It was three days before they removed her restraints. It felt good to rub her tender skin, even better to see her sister was allowed up and moving about her room. Today was the first day for their training and Vee was beyond nervous. After all of the blood work and mental evaluations they had done to her and Lita; was it really worth it.

“Andrevenya, we are ready for you.” A young nurse said with a soft smile.

Vee turned to see Lolita was already making her way down the hall. A white gown billowing against the silver metal of her wheelchair. A pretty white ghost with dark hair floating along the dim hallways.

Her heart began to race as she went further down the winding halls, passing creatures you’d only see in horror films. Scaly beasts that hissed behind muzzles, snapping at Lolita ahead of her, who only moved away and was kept going by the swarm of doctors and nurses clustered around them both. Young, sweet looking little girls whose heads turned round like the owl in the forest searching for its prey and Vee would constantly feel like the mouse.

The tall gray doors hissed as they parted. Concentrated air floated along her feet in white clouds, making her step aside from the sudden chill. Without being able to even exchange a glance, the girls were ushered into two separate rooms.

Lolita sat in the changing room. A black bundle of fabric sat clutched in her hands. She could make out the mesh material but the slick material was foreign to her. She removed the white thin dress and tossed it in what she thought was a laundry bin. The bright flash that exploded from the opening and burning sound that crackled from it as the gown slipped through really answered her question; it was an incinerator. Slipping the body suit on, she realized it was practically stitched to her skin it was to form fitting. And yet, it was very comfortable and gave her tons of flexibility. The mesh ran down her arms to her wrists and the silky slick material covered her torso and parts of her thighs before the mesh reappeared in certain areas such as parts of her thighs and stomach around to her back, showing off the spine long scar residing there.

She looked powerful in the suit. Lolita liked it. All her life she felt weak and now, she was about to expose her raw power and show that she can finally hold her own. No more backing down. She wasn't going to have to have someone else stick up for her in her own fights.

Wheeling out of the changing room, she found herself in a large, white, dome shaped arena. Lights scattered under the floor along the edges and Vee was pacing ahead of her, slowly turning on her heels staring at how high the building climbed. They had to be pretty far down in the earth for them to not even be able to see the roofing.

"Lolita? Andrevenya?" The sisters spun around.

A young woman with shocking blue hair that ombred to fuschia approached them. It fell in long ringlets on the right side of her humble face. The side shave she had was appropriately colored. Her ears were decorated in silver metal and bright blue eyeshadow messily decorated her sharp eyes. One eye was a machine, a robotic eye with glowing mechanics and gears. The white mesh body suit hugged her with every step she took approaching the girls.

“The name’s Karis and I’m your guy’s instructor. The scientists have analyzed every last nerve in your bodies and blood cell. So, I have a whole list of abilities we need to work on unleashing mmmkay?” She chirped with a brief smile on unreal, glossy lips.

“Andrevenya-”

Vee held up her hand to halt the strange girl.

“You can call me Vee.”

“And I like to go by Lita,” her younger sister spoke up from behind her.

“Alrighty, well. Vee, your powers.” She said pulling out a tablet and typing a few codes onto the screen.

“Ah, here we go. Your powers are all energy and nature based, we can only assume that's because of the time period you were born they thought it would fit best. Aerokinesis which means you have the power to manipulate the air and wind to bend to your will however you plan to use it. Your lungs can be trained to adapt in different situations. This is saying there is a thin film over your lungs that grew there like a parasite and if we can get that peeled off the lung and make it its own organism, it can filter out any toxic particles in the air you breathe. Making mustard gas a thing of your past, for example." She chuckled before clearing her throat awkwardly and continued.

"Uhmm, oh! You have the ability to where you can sense, create, shape and manipulate weather, called Atmokinesis. You said you caught something on fire yes?"

Vee nodded, her emotions colliding with her words in the middle of her neck. She coughed and nodded.

"Yes, I set a fire in my kitchen." She felt a soft and small hand squeeze hers from behind.

"Well, that is what becomes of your anger. You're so strongly built on emotion that it needs to be controlled and focused or else you could bring about more harm than just a few burnt appliances. Its called fire manipulation where your body can conjure up enough gas particles and liquid pulled from your water intake to change it to a form of gasoline.

Basically you can conjure up fire or become a walking fire yourself; called inflammation. You can also- teleport by self explosion into a million molecules and only are held by thin strands of atoms to move about our world undetected. Then you have simple powers such as freezing and breathing under water and shapeshifting into living creatures that are not human." Karis smiled closing the file on the tablet.

"Any questions before I move onto Lita?"

A welcome silenced followed. Karis took the hint and clicked her tongue softly before opening up the second file and sighed taking a deep breath.

"Ok, Lita… You ready?" She asked with a raise of her sharply sculpted brow.

Lolita nodded, unsure after hearing just how powerful Vee really could become. Would she ever match up?

"Well, for starters; your powers are more mechanic and technology based. Considering you were born when? Two thousand?"

Lolita nodded again, throat dry.

"Yeah, that's what I thought. And while Vee's abilities are activated and strongest when her emotions are in full throttle; yours are at their strongest peak when you *lack* every sense of emotional connection to the world. Technology cannot process emotion, so you can't either if you want to win a fight. You have the basics like night vision, invisibility and teleportation in a similar way Vee transports. But the big powers we need to work on are like this one," she said tapping a little link on the screen.

"Electrokinesis, the definition of being able to bend and create electric voltage between the palms of your hand, and while Vee can morph into a body of flames, you can do the same just as a form of electrical energy in its purest form. You can also absorb electricity if you can't create it yourself given the circumstance you are in. Kind of a sneak attack sorta move. And your final ability; Mechanical Intuition. It is where your mind connects and functions like the world's smartest computer, being able to intuitively understand the operation of any mechanical device and effortlessly create a schematic in your mind to create or understand any mechanical device."

Karis smiled, proud of herself and tucked the device away, staring up at the slack jawed girls.

"Shall we begin?"

The sisters exchanged an uneasy look, but nodded at their teacher. Karis nodded and backed up, grabbing a small remote. She clicked it and the room went black, except for the floor lights providing quite the flickering light show.

" Level one," a robotic woman's voice spoke through the surround sound speakers.

The lights snapped on and the sisters were surrounded by hooded figures gripping guns, blades and whips. Their faces were a dark and empty void.

Computer programmed. Lolita thought to herself.

Alright, I'll play

Bullets flew in every direction. Bodies flung themselves quick as the metals fired. Whips lashed out; snapping against the air. Vee centered her mind on one thing; protect Lita.

She felt the rush of every electron in her body jumping their energy levels until she erupted with a bright white light shining from her core. In a burst of red hot particles she was gone. All in a nanosecond, she could feel herself one with the air. Her vision was fast; nauseatingly fast. The invaders were hazy and blending images as she soared fast as the speed of light. She reappeared in her solid form to grow a set of eagle talons to slice off the head of three hooded figures. Their bodies exploded into thousands of black glass shards.

They aren't real.

Oh where's the fun in that?

She had to admit, the thrill of these emotions gathering together and mixing unevenly inside her to bring out this double persona was thrilling. Addictive and she wanted to taste more.

Lolita was halfway across the area, her body now a sparking embodiment of electrical energy. Her white eyes all void of colors scanned the large room; laying out a grid and putting each figure on a pin point. Spheres of high volts gathered in her palms and as one went to crack the leather across her sisters' unsuspecting back, she released the energy. The being withered and rolled on the soft floor in utmost agony. She remained dead to empathy's cries. The human within sobbed for the tortuous death this being had brought to the unreal figure, she chose to ignore it for now; knowing full well if she gave in all the strength she had to protect her loved one, will disappear.

Vee backed away from the being as it became a pile of black glass. Something hard struck her in the back anyway. A hooded figure raised its large hand; fully intending on ripping her ribs from her chest through her spinal cord. In brief haste; she clutched the closest piece of glass, contorted her body around to stab the creature deep in the jugular.

Only two remained. A final meal for each.

Lita was no longer a body of energy, but her sweet little self sitting in her wheelchair as the “Person” stalked and circled her. A sword swinging back and forth in an obviously skilled hand. The map appeared in her eyes again, calculating every step he took, breath and pulse in his wrist. Her eyes flickered above them and when he got the hint and looked up, it was too late for him. The giant piece of equipment that had been hanging above them since they arrived in the area came loose of its cables and begun to fall. It crushed the imaginative figure before it could raise an arm to even attempt in protecting itself.

All that remained was the last invader closing in on Vee and Lita tried to advance and help her, a digital net closed her in. This was not her fight. Understanding; she backed away from the hexagonal fencing that generated out of thin air.

The creature was strong. It pushed Vee with one outstretched palm, sending her slamming into the plexiglass where scientists stood unfazed and monitoring the girls vitals and work that may need improved. Completely oblivious to her pain as she slid down the wall.

She grunted and hoisted herself to kneel on one leg, her arms splayed out for balance. Her chest burned where he had pushed. Her bones there felt broken, but it could also be numbing adrenaline not being enough of a sedative.

Standing up, she growled like a wolf and so; that is what she became. The sound of bones snapping and bending mercilessly to take shape of the creature was enough to make Lita gag and cover her mouth. Her sister's once beautiful short and choppy hair covered her body, parts standing out sharp as little needles. Soft hands became paws and six inch claws ready to peel and skin ripe flesh. Her white pearly teeth lengthened to sharp canines and those soft understanding amber eyes with gold flecks were a deep red from tear duct clear across the sclera. Vee was taller than any dog she had ever seen. She could be rode into battle. Shoulder blades were higher than her head if she could stand up.

A monster.

The beast stalked the figure whom merely stepped in the perfect circle, raising the blade letting the light catch it and glare in the red eyes. Taunting her and it was a fatal game.

Wasting no time, the wolf launched herself on the man, pinning him down with ease. The claws made hom in the chest ripping out the beating heart. It continued to beat for a few mere seconds as it was tossed aside and rolled on the floor before crippling into black ashes. The gaping chest cavity oozed a black liquid that could only be assumed of as this fake beings blood. The wolf licked it with her tongue. The acidic saliva boiled and melted the skin it touched like hot candle wax.

The program showed the figure mercy and it dissipated in black glass and ashes. The wolf snarled at the remains, huffing so they blew away and spread across the once pristine floor. Now littered in neat piles of black.

The net faded away and Lolita fearlessly moved to the wolf. She knew her sister wouldn't harm her no matter the form or state she was in. She was right, for the wolf twisted its bones and in a matter of seconds the snarling beast was now her heaving sister. Hands drenched in black blood. Looking at her sister, hands holding her coated ones, all she could think to say in a trembling voice on the border of a nervous laugh was;

"When this is all over, I want my sanity back."

The sisters rested their foreheads together and broke into laughter. They actually did it. Protected one another in so many insane ways and were stronger than they each anticipated. Above all; the abilities worked in every beneficial way. That deserved a nice ice cream sundae and maybe some wine.

"Congrats on passing the easiest level we could make without consulting a toddler to design it." Karis chimed from above them.

She landed on her feet after falling nearly a story and a half. Walking towards the sisters, she helped Vee rise to her feet from her kneeled position; a glitter in her one human eye.

"Ready to go again?"

One in the morning was when they finally were escorted out of the area, leaving behind the guns and blades littering its floors. Vee sat on her twin bed. The mattress dipping beneath her weight and the pillows plump and ready for to rest her head for the next few hours before it was to start all over again like clockwork. A solo touch lamp was dimly casting a cool glow in her eyes as she watched the digits tick by on the digital clock attached. The pod was small, but she wasn't claustrophobic. She enjoyed tiny spaces for it always opened her mind to really be forced to think. Adjusting her black tank top's strap back onto her aching shoulder, she managed to stand up. Everything hurt. The adrenaline had worn off and she had to face the fact she was still human and pain was not a thing of her past.

She missed Rick. Whenever she was in pain, whether it be a migraine or a bruise she somehow acquired at work, he was always there. Medicine in one hand, while the other had already been set with preparing the bed and warm rags. She missed the massages he would give her temples with her head in his lap as she cried into the night from the undying pain. How he would grow so upset that he couldn't help her, but tried his hardest to make her comfortable. A single tear ran down her cheek as she stared back at her reflection in the glass pod door. Through the thin layer of fog from her, she saw Lolita's petite outline across the silent hall. She slept peacefully in her own pod without sorrow, without heartache.

Andrevenya knew, Rick had to fade away. He had more to worry about, more to care about. The fog cleared away with the coolness of the oxygen hissing from the pod door as it opened.

"Hey, Vee."

She looked up seeing Danny in her doorway. Two beers in his hand.

"I know the nurses said no alcohol and I won't be giving you this until you promise not to use it as a weapon," her friend said with that oh so cute playful grin.

She nodded and the cool glass was in her outstretched hand. The condensation dripping through the lines in her fingers. Looping his now free arms under her elbow, they left the hallway of sleeping pods and down a few halls before resting on a bench. Her eyes weren't focused on that.

Her eyes were on the stars.

In front of the little metal bench was a wall of glass. It was full of the galaxy. On the background made of rich navy and dotted white stars was a wisp. She was beautiful. Twisted smoke, ice and stones twirling as her tail was bursting with teal and white light.

The smoke continued to circle her tail made of ice and cosmic dust.

“Cosmos redshift seven,” Danny said as he watched his friend stare in wonder at the beauty before her.

“ It’s just an image, because some people down here need something from the outside world to see, why not go so outside the world that it’s no longer ours. But one of billions that we share such a small portion of, that we are practically nonexistent to the stronger forces lying just beyond us out there, somewhere.” He whispered as she sat beside him.

“Like other worlds?” She asked as she set down the drink beside her feet, not caring about the liquid anymore.

“Well yeah. We can’t just be the only ones here. If we alone were able to create something and marvelously alien such as you; certainly even greater things have to be out there impacting our lives.”

Her eyes faltered down before looking back at him.

"Why didn't you tell me that you knew, Danny? I thought we trusted one another."

A small sigh escaped him. He wished they could just avoid it all.

"Because you wouldn't have. Trust me, that is. If I came to you and told you I knew you could shapeshift, turn into a ball of fire for christ sake, or even explode and reanimate in another location, would you believe me?" He pleaded.

Silence.

Vee looked down at her lap, feeling the tears well behind her eyes before sharply releasing her held breath and staring at the galaxy once more. Her messy ringlets flew off her face and settled against the nape of her neck.

"No, guess I wouldn't have."

They sat there in quietness. The awkward tense fading away as a shooting star soared across the digital screen panels.

“How is the training going for you two?” He took a swig and waited for her response.

“We are advancing faster than they can prepare. It hasn’t even been a day and we have mastered every ability in us. They will be releasing us in the morning and will call when they feel its time to go to the lab.”

She could not believe this was her reality now. Sneaking to a foreign country where she was-- invented to gather information that may or may not even be there.

“Literally everything about your guy’s plan is illegal.” She said with a dead expression. She knew she wasn’t wrong and she silently dared this man to fight her otherwise.

“We never said you had to Vee! Keep your powers use them for good. Keep Lolita close. Have that family you’ve always wanted.” He laughed cheerfully. He only ever wanted the best for his best friend no matter what she may be.

“Because,” her voice strained and she had to clear her throat and calm herself.

“Because if I go through with this, we could die. If I don’t; everyone will die.”

His smile only brightened as he held her hand in his own.

“Now that, is the what a hero would say.”

She jerked her hand away as if it burned.

“I’m not a hero. I just can’t go on with life knowing any second I could be the one thing to end everyone else's. Karis told me about this Luca man who created the formula to make us. He’s still in Tobolsk?”

“He tends to move around quite a bit. But currently he is in France and we can’t send you there. So, Karis wanted me to give you this,” he handed her a large envelop and she pulled out its contents.

“House key to a townhouse in Brooklyn a quick drive from here. Hollenbeck will have the portions in the hospital funding be sent out to pay every expense you may have. We can't risk you two having a job. That's how they caught you last time." He explained.

She looked up at him and with a watery smile, she said. "Thank you. For everything. Being here, for understanding and willing to help me- us out."

Danny said nothing. He pulled her into a tight hug. She wrapped her arms around him as she took deep breaths.

The world had a lot in store. She wasn't sure that she was ready.

Chapter 10

"Lita you don't get the master bedroom."

"But my room is smaller than my other one back in Florida… In both homes I lived in."

"It is *literally* the same size."

After being with her for almost four months, this was the first fight Vee ever had with Lolita. It was a petty one, but she was glad it was that way. It shows their strong bond that had to be there after all they've been through. And a fight over a space between four walls, well, she was more than happy to argue over that.

Her sister scowled and flung herself back into the task of unpacking the little she had out of beaten up boxes.

"After we are done, can we at least go shopping? Or out to grab something to eat?" The little pout on her lips was enough to warm Vee's heart.

Lolita reminded her lot of how she was at her age. Bratty at times, but irresistible and you could never stay mad for long. Because she always wanted to make it up to you.

“ Sure, let’s head on out. I know a good burger joint just down the street. We could even walk there.” Vee called over her shoulder,froze and spun around with a bruised look on her wincing face.

“I’m sorry- I didn’t-”

“It’s fine really. These legs need some toning. I mean,” She looked down and placed a hand on her calf. The skin limp beneath her. “Have you seen them? These poor suckers need some toning ASAP!” Lita laughed and placed her hands back on the box, sliding it down the hall before turning back to Vee. “Let’s get going, I’m starving.”

“Alright. Burger, no onions and a small seasoned fry on the side. That will be nine dollars, seventy-one cents.” Lolita rolled her eyes but slapped the money on the sticky counter.

Why make it so expensive? It really doesn’t look like anything that special, not hers, or Vee’s as she sat behind her at the table by the wide spanning window.

Because it's New York, living the dream kid. Vee's voice whispered in her head.

Taking the tray to her lap, the teenager wheeled herself to the table where Vee was already diving into the half eaten burger.

"No onions? Don't tell me you're the weaker sister." Vee joked at her sister's mere eye roll being her response.

"Don't even start. Now," Lita's voice dropped as she slid aside the meal and took a sip of her water, "about this Luca guy Danny told me about."

"Lita, why did you have to mention him? I'm trying to enjoy my lunch." The sister whined.

"But, Hollenbeck did call late last night about that."

"And?" Lita asked, eagerly munching down on the hot fries that scalded her tongue.

"They were able to get some video and Luca is back in Tobolsk. They want us to head out as soon as we are settled in."

Vee began to dive back into the still hot food, but hunger escaped Lolita as she nudged the tray further from her. They could be spending this time doing far better things for them. Like reconnecting to make up for the lost time they never had together. Bonding over their love for life under the sea. The mysteries and dumb conspiracies of the world. But no, instead they got to haul up what they owned and hide away in the city like the roaches under the streets. Hiding like fools from utterly mad scientists who have done to them what the masses would consider pure science fiction. Untrue, false, worthy of being thrown into a padded cell and watch the key be melted down before their eyes. Never to see the light of day again.

"Lita, we need to go."

Lolita rose her head, their senses heightening together almost instantaneously at the bustle of people around them. Andrevenya set down her Styrofoam cup and her eyes set on Lolita's, like steel.

"What do you feel?" Lolita asked as she felt the energies radiating from the others body.

"We have a shadow. Let's go."

The two wasted no time and were out of the diner heading back to the apartment. They could see it looming among the other skyscrapers running against the clouds overhead. Vee could feel the energy growing stronger behind them and she spun around. Inches. from the two girls was one around her sister's age. Her hair was wild with curls around her face and a calm expression rested on her features.

"Hi, I'm Jade Ryan." The New York native said bluntly and extended her hand to Vee. When she saw the two weren't buying into it, she lowered it, mumbling something like, *well okay then*, under her breath awkwardly.

"Well, Jade." Lolita spoke up with darkness outlining her eyes. " Wanna explain why you were following us?"

"I live right down the hall from you guys and I live with my grandmother. I noticed the night you two moved in that you had quite the muscles packed in those teeny arms ya two got there."

The sisters exchanged a glance. Wide eyed, lips parted before the muscles in each tensed til it hurt.

They were so dead.

"W-what did you see, exactly?" Lolita asked, her voice craning in her neck.

"Just that *you* had turned into a ball of light and she," Her eyes turned their attention of Vee.

" Had decided to literally turn into a cat to put something on a high shelf before exploding like a grenade had been Kobe'd at her, re appearing before my eyes as a person, and then continued to sit there while you set up a television with full on surround sound, I might add, in under sixty seconds. Not only to mention the fact you conjured up a store bought DVD player out of mid air with lint, string and a paperclip...Paper. Clip!"

When the three had begun getting stares from New Yorkers, it meant it was quite crazy what they were hearing. And they are from New York City. Vee grabbed this Jade by one arm and Lolita followed suit. They fought up the down running river of people until they were in a small crevice between two buildings.

“What will it take to make sure you don’t tell a soul.” Lolita snarled lowly at the unfazed teen leaning casually against the wall before her.

“A friendship. You two seem wicked cool.”

Is this girl bipolar?

Shut up.

Vee shook her head and pinched the bridge of her nose, exhaling as calmly as she could with the building stress.

“I mean come on! It’s like I’d be making friends with comic book heroes! Or do you prefer anti heroes? You kinda share that grungy vibe, ya know?” Jade chuckled, not noticing the total shock on the girls faces.

“You just want us to all be friends?” Lolita tilted her head to the side.

"Yeah? Is that like a crime against the supernatural beings club or something?" The girl asked her.

"Well, no." Vee stepped in clearing her throat, "but you can't tell anyone got it?"

Jade only drew her finger across thin lips.

"My lips are sealed." She deadpanned before breaking into a soft laugh, clapping her hands.

"Oh my god, this is gonna be so much fun!"

The sisters both looked up and down at one another. These just made things a whole lot worse, didn't it?

"Woah, this place is so cool!" Jade gasped and dropped her school bag to the floor, gawking at the large penthouse apartment.

Well she wasn't wrong. The large flat screen tv mounted on the wall with every video game box set imaginable organized neatly in a glass and sleek black bordered cabinet underneath. The minimalistic yet rich furnishings placed accordingly throughout the room such as industrial stage lights casting a dazzling sparkle on the glass dining room table and sterling white chairs balancing on chrome legs diagonal from the large L shaped leather couch decked out in matching black cushions decked out around the glass coffee table facing the tv center piece.

Jade walked over and sat down on a soft and fluffy black cushion, turning on the massive tv as it came to life with bright and vivid color.

"How did you guys pay for all of this?"

" A lot of help," Vee mumbled under her breath as she made her way to the industrial modern kitchen that sat to the side of the massive open space. She needed a drink and desperately.

Lita wheeled over to Jade and collapsed herself out of her wheelchair and onto the soft leather waiting for her there. Her little body seemed to sink under the feather like weight of the couch seat. She loved it. Jade stared over at the girl and squinted her eyes.

"So, what exactly are you guys? Mutants or something?"

“Something like that,” Lolita responded with a low tiredness in her voice. The day was a long one and she did not feel up for idle chat. “An experiment gone horribly wrong.”

This captured Jade’s attention as she spun away from the television and faced the girl lying on her stomach sinking into the couch as if she were some wide goddess struck down from the heavens to deliver her tale.

“Tell me,” she pleaded with her as Vee returned with hot chocolate in her hand, brandy mixed in the milky chocolate while sitting beside her sister's limp body. The fatigue overcoming them both simultaneously

“A science lab in a far away country had created us in hopes we could destroy the world under their command. We would have no choice and be powerless to their strong hand.” Lolita said monotone as her eyes seemed to drift elsewhere in the universe. Lost to the world as she shared their story.

"What country?" Jade asked, her eyes could grow no larger and her ears absorbed the story like a massive sponge to an endless body of water.

"Russia. They had decided it would be best to protect their people from any enemies and or threats by destroying the entire planet with two biological weapons that couldn't possibly be detected by any metal detectors, radiation or nuclear scanning since it was mixed in with the smallest particles of DNA in the human body. Undetectable by anything other than those who know of our creation."

"Woah," Jade whispered and Vee snorted quietly to herself.

Why would any normal person believe the tale Lolita was saying. This Jade couldn't be normal then. Vee knew she wouldn't of believed this insane story if she was not a part of it so intricately. She sipped her concoction as Lolita hummed quietly to herself, eyes fluttered shut. But Jade was not done with her interrogation just yet.

"Can you guys show me your powers?"

Silence.

"Oh come one! I won't tell anyone and besides, I only got to see it from far away. You already told me your life story why not just keep going? Too deep now to just pull away." Jade snapped Lolita from her groggy state and she sighed to herself, glancing up at her sister who frowned even though upside down in her eyes.

But, the two finally gave in.

What possible harm could it do in the safe confines of a guarded apartment with Hollenbeck's security on every floor?

Speaking of security; Vee had to talk to them about allowing a seventeen or sixteen year old come into such close contact with them in their own building complex when they were specifically hired to prevent this exact thing from happening.

Vee was first to move. She stood up and with a steady look in her eyes, her fingers flicked to one side. A single, small ember began to glow at her manicured nails. The infant flame danced along her fingers. It twirled up the length then jumping from one finger and down to her pinkie before soaring from the tender skin and onto the wick of a waiting candle. The little ember blossomed into a beautiful singular flame on the candle and the wax began to heat.

Jade was entranced by the gorgeous act that displayed itself before her. The room was soft spare for the occasional crack as the wick broke down under the intensifying heat.

"My body identifies with the natural energies of our world." Vee explained after the silence had played its role long enough.

Lolita took the statement as her cue and casually held up her fingers, Strong bolts of electric energy flowed from them and she bent forward to touch the remote sitting so neatly on the coffee table. The sparks flew from its sensor right on the TV before them. The screen changed images at rapid pace. Faster than any electronic could go in their day and age. It settled on a nature display. The honeysuckles dancing in the calm summer breeze. She lifted her nails from the remote and sent the energy flowing within her at the lights. Their hue of warm daylight changed to a calming red, then to sparking blue, green, yellow. The range was endless as she bent the color fragments within the lights waves with no effort at all. The rainbow strobe was marvelous, to say the least.

"My body is only in tune with our ever changing technology when my heart and mind are vacant of any emotion. Then, and only then, can I become the world's fastest and smartest computer. Able to do whatever I desire, whenever I want to do so. Hack into the pentagon as I sip the morning coffee, relocate a Navy submarine with the flick of my wrist simply because I was bored." The young woman explained to the slack jawed teen sitting in front of her.

Jade had to gather said jaw from the floor and swallowed thickly. She had assumed they were supernatural humans, but never to such a strong degree. She had just come to realize she just befriended the strongest women known to science. Defied every science she or Einstein himself would ever know.

"Do you think, if they found a way to reverse these powers and you could be normal again? Would you do it?" She asked them.

The sisters stared at one another before turning back to the girl.

"No." They said in unison.

"Because, like my wheelchair," Lolita continued, " it is what ironically, makes me stand out. It is how I found my family. I wouldn't trade this for all the riches that anyone could offer me."

"And what is normal anyway? An illusion of comfort? A typical state of mind society forces into our minds at young, impressionable ages? I believe normal never can, or will ever, exist. There will always be a sense of mystery, a false understanding and an endless journey to find yourself that will always be different than your neighbor, your brother or your parents." Vee finished as she sipped her drink once more.

The clock on the far wall ticked by the eternity lasting minutes before Jade received a text from her grandmother to come home finally.

When Jade had left, Lolita curled her body close to Vee's and fell asleep there. Deciding to no longer sit in silence, the tv was providing her numbing entertainment through the early hours of the setting sun. Soft ocres and blazing reds casted themselves through the window that stretched from wall to wall and onto every light struck corner of the space. Navy blue and black clouds dashed across the sky by God's paintbrush and the sun was beginning to hide behind the inky clouds lying at the horizon.

Sleep plagued the back of her mind, but the ringing of her phone lulled her back to the land of the living. Looking at the clock she saw it was already almost ten at night. The sunset was vacant and only blue stars remained in the night sky.

Grabbing the phone, she saw it was her special doctor and opened up the call.

"Vee, glad you decided to pick up. This is the third time I tried to reach you tonight." He grumbled on the other end.

"Don't start sounding like a poor schoolboy crush on me now. Not picking up whenever you ring me."

The woman smirked as her knees rested under her chin, blankly watching the now muted television as a dumb sitcom played on.

"Very funny. But tomorrow I need you and Lita on a plane to Moscow. The window is very narrow. He's back in Russia but, nowhere near the lab so you can retrieve the information only by the time you get there and only a few hours at that."

"Well, then why not just wait until there's a bigger window?" She asked confused, being sure to stay quiet lest she wake her sister.

"Because if we wait for a next window, there will be no next window. He plans to destroy the old lab and wants to take any information including the working formula and create a whole army of weapons. Now that he knows you two were successes." Grant explained as calmly as he could manage.

Vee sighed and ran her fingers through her slightly tangled hair. Could she really do this? Something so illegal as breaking and entering to steal tons of old files on dangerous world ending weapons to give to a doctor who doesn't even work for any government, but for unknown creatures hidden away miles beneath the world from sight?

Apparently so, because she agreed to go the next morning and woke Lolita to tell her the plan.

Morning came and the girls were gone from the apartment. Gone from the safety of the seemingly bodiless security they were so good at being invisible and gone from Jade before she could hunt them down and be a distraction and gone before the sun could show its face.

The car ride to the JFK airport was quiet. Mainly for the fact Lolita was still sound asleep in the tiled back passenger seat. Traffic wasn't too bad for three thirty in the morning. Still a hustle and bustle, but not car stopping traffic on the streets. Parking was a hassle for Vee and she just felt like making one explode so she could park in the filled handicapped spots. Most of them didn't even have a sticker anywhere in or on the vehicles. With Lolita awake, she was able to get one of those spots, thanks to her little companion moving the Ferrari to a spot three parking levels up.

TSA was annoying to Lolita as they waited in the relatively short line. No, in fact, she hated them with a burning passion. When she was six years old; she Hallie and Claudia had planned a trip to Las Vegas and they obviously wanted to get there as soon as possible. So, a plane was the only choice. The employees there treated her like she was going to carry six bombs on her and in the wheelchair. Her family got off somewhat clean, until they found out about their Hispanic heritage and then it was a train wreck. All the scanning and full body checks. Lolita was still scarred after the heavy female woman forced her back brace off her tiny body and did a… thorough sweep, to say the least. Now, as she became third in line, second in line; she could only imagine how this round will go. Considering she had no hard plaster brace covering her torso to protect her a few seconds longer or the fact she was now almost an adult woman.

"Next."

Here goes nothing.

Vee was on the other side, gathering her items from the bins that had gone through the x-ray checks. She now was scooping up

Lita's items as she watched her paralyzed sister be pushed against her rightful will to go behind a screen a ways away. She knew Lolita despised it when people pushed her wheelchair. It stripped her of dignity and independence. The minutes were turtle slow. She could only anxiously wait for her sister as two officers checked her wheelchair and body. As if she was carrying a weapon. It made Vee scoff at the thought.

You don't need a weapon when you were born one.

After decades of the waiting, Lolita appeared from behind the thick screen and hurried over to her sister with an unreadable look plastered on her sullen face. Vee didn't pry. It wasn't her place. If Lolita wanted to talk about her experiences in anything, she would tell her once she felt comfortable enough to.

Gate 34H.

They still had time before the plane would even arrive into sighted air space, let alone land, unboard, clean out, then board passengers. So, while Vee slouched in a nearby chair, resting her chin in her palm watching mindless youtube videos on her phone, Lita took the chance to explore the massive airport.

She got the typical stares from young children and idiot adults as she fearlessly wheeled past them. With all the strength at her fingertips, she feared no one. Her eyes wavered about the airport. Endless rows of food establishments in the food courts, shops and pharmacies even. Nothing of any real interest to her. She didn't have much time left to explore either.

Finally, at the end of the massive airport was a small room. A large glowing cross stood proudly above her and the double doors. Lolita never was a super religious girl. Sure she believed in higher beings but never truly agreed with all in that belief. But, she had time to kill.

“Amen” The priest ducked his head away from the congregation of five lost souls and one who wasn’t supposed to have one.

The majority fearing the high skies they were about to endure, or the upcoming meetings they were dreading at the end of their trip high above the world.

Lolita sat as far away from the altar or priest as she possibly could. She was nowhere near a vampire, but feared she would be treated the same way. A freak of nature, a time bomb ready to kill millions while sitting and defying everything the church held dear and taught to the people.

"Are you alright, my child?" A man of ninety years spoke up and Lolita jumped.

The priest did bring her a fatherly atmosphere with him as he sat in the pew beside her wheelchair that stuck out in the aisle like a sore thumb. She always did wish she could of have grown up with a real dad, but that was never going to be in the cards for her.

"I'm just going through a lot, Father." She added in quickly, remembering whom she was speaking to.

"Go on, my child."

She exhaled shaky and wrung her hands together as her eyes darted around the small dimly lit room.

"At times, I- I just seem to morph into this raging, tortured creature that I just can't always control."

The priest, a poor man, wrung his own hands together with his voice a mess of stuttering and stammering.

"I am no expert dear on this topic. But, I do believe that this is something normal for girls or ladies around your age."

Lolita scoffed.

"Not the time you're thinking of. I can't seem to get this one saying out of my head, Father. When I was in the pitch black room, the flies resting on the carcass; it sang to me. Roses are wilting, the violets are crying. You aren't in the hospital. They are saying that you're dying… What could that possibly mean, Father?"

There was a look of worry and fear in the old man's worn eyes. The creases in his face only seemed to deepen as he hurriedly excused himself. The girl took this chance to leave the small church.

Some people are just so gullible.

Before she left, her eyes moved back to see the sculpture. The Lord hanging by the wooden cross above the altar. She raised a brow at it.

"Oh, don't look at me like that. I'm not even human. So don't expect a demon to show compassion."

And with that, she made her way back to her sister. They had a flight to catch.

Chapter 11

Hollenbeck really went all out. Putting the girls in first class in the most comfortable aircraft was like a vacation. A vacation that could result in them getting killed or worse, but a vacation nonetheless. Vee held a satchel on her lap with white knuckles. While Lolita had gone off on her little adventure a few hours earlier, Danny had actually stopped by and had given her this; a bag containing different identification and typical women's clothing fit for Russia. A long shawl to protect their faces and head from the whipping winds the season wrought throughout the tundra and heavy gowns to layer beneath it.

The world was foggy against the thick window pane. The sun rising on the other side. The snow capped city appeared from the thin clouds as she felt the craft lower to greet the icy land. Large domes on the churches and other buildings reminded Vee of candies and it made her smirk. Had she not have a distaste for the country and its past leaders,she would find the place stunning and worthy of exploring and learning. No time for touring, they had work to do.

Domodedovo Airport. It was beautiful; Lolita took in its beauty and large crowds of people rushing by. They had just left the ladies room, now blending in to the masses in the shawls and thick fabrics weighing them both down.

They gained no suspicious looks or side glances, so the looks must be working. After all, most of the clothes covered the majority of their faces. Lolita's mind kicked in and analyzed every sign, translating the jumbled foreign letters into perfect English. It is what lead them right out the front door a few floors below. Clutching the bag to her side, Vee didn't bother flagging down a cab, taxi or car. Instead the two ventured out to the streets of Moscow. It was going to be a few train rides to Tobolsk.

The train rides were bumpy and extremely uncomfortable. Sickness seemed to spread with every word the people spoke around them. If Vee got sick she swore she was going to explode without the help of a trigger.

But now, as they strolled along the side roads on partial asphalts roads, she felt as though she could breathe again. Pale pink bricks built up the homes dotting the otherwise barren roads, save for the single old car that would lurch on by.

Each home in the countryside they were traveling looked nearly the same. Lolita did catch glimpses of children playing behind high walls of backyards and puppies chasing after them joyfully before crashing into hills of snow built up.

They knew they were getting close by mid day when they saw the pretty brick homes gradually fade into old shacks made with splintering and decaying wooden planks with broken windows. Karis had informed them that the lab was set in the middle of seemingly nowhere in the rural slummy part of Tobolsk on purpose. To ease the suspicion of the higher living locals. They stopped to rest on a little side row beside a small dropping cliff to let Vee lean against.

“This is the largest country in the world and Grant expects us to find a small laboratory in it with the only scale down he gave us what it being that it's in one huge city!” Vee shouted angrily at the sky, but was hushed by Lolita’s stern hiss.

"Hey, wanna scream in English any louder and get us caught when we are trying to blend in?" Her younger sister snapped softly before looking around.

The rural area was a flat stone of dead grass becoming a calm sea when the wind blew. She hugged the shawl tighter to her face, shielding it from the harsh whipping air. Something caught eyé. It was a shimmering object.

A glass bottle perhaps? Wheeling away from Vee whom was surveying the area for herself, she went closer and found a shard of a window laying in the soft white. Another piece was not too far away, leading up a cobblestone ramp along the cliff side they were just resting against. The moss poked out from the snow and wood fragments decorated the pillowing green. Shredded wet paper clung to the cobblestone. Following the peculiar path, her eyes rose from the rubble.

"Vee," she hissed and got no response. Rolling her eyes she hollered louder.

"Andrevenya!"

That got her attention, for seconds later she was clamoring her way up the stony trail. They said nothing as they stared at the vacant house before them. The white paint peeled away from the outer walls of the one story building showing off the ashy brick beneath, the metal roofing already caving in from the snow's weight.

Vee stepped forward, snow and glass crunching beneath her boot. Touching the old iron door, it creaked open weakly. The sun weakly lit the space and she turned back to her sister. She nodded and the two faded inside.

Destruction. That was the best way Vee could put it in her jumbled mind. Papers spilling from blue folders scattered the dusty wood floors. Tables turned over, staining the floor with age old coffee from broken mugs. The air reeked of dead animals in the walls and wet floor planks rotting beneath their feet and wheels. The sun shone through dust and dead insect covered windows.

Lolita felt she was either going to vomit, or catch a disease of a sort in the grave of a building. Instead, she forced herself to wheel over to a bookshelf. An assortment of waterlogged books sat there. The titles ranged from human anatomy, to fairytales.

Scanning over the novels, one caught her eye and she reached for it. She stopped and quickly put on her thick gloves, then grabbed the book and removed it from the shelf.

There was a deadly groan and it rattled the bones in the sisters. Hinges turned on their last limb. The last books sank to the floor and some disintegrated before her eyes. The dead air tossing the damp ashes aside. The sisters looked at one another in shock as an elevator was revealed with a set of stairs. Many metal planks missing. Pushing the button, the elevator obeyed almost instantly. Rotting gold embellishments reminiscent of what once was. She winced as the floorboard groaned under her wheelchairs weight. Vee stepped in after and pressed the floor one button. The doors shut in front of them and the creaking sound of a dead violin began to play its haunting melody. The atmosphere drowned in a ghosted past plaguing the small building they found themselves trapped within. They hit rock bottom with a sharp jolt and the doors behind them parted tiredly.

Lolita turned around and her eyes took it all in. A chrome room filled to the brim with their beginnings. Long tables littered with microscopes, documents. Along the one wall was age old computers and another stacked to the limit in files, VHS tapes and floppy disks. Black boards with over a hundred formulas scrawled along from left to right. Some hastily erased and written over in another way or style. Large tubes stood proud on the tables a few feet away from the messy boards. Along the tube siding inside were dried remains of organs and once liquid material. The oxygen was a thin haze across the ceiling and Lolita could only assume it was due to the released decaying materials so carelessly left behind. Worn tape hung loosely to the last bit of strength it had to the clear tubes, each marked in sharpie a scribble of symbols. Lolita leaned in to translate while Vee ventured to the files and date packed away on the walls and in the extinct computer's hard drives.

"They're numbered." Lolita whispered, her breath fogging the glass as her nail pulled at the strips of tape.

"Here's 2459," she gasped and examined the tube.

It was mechanical and held shut with an air tight lid. She touched the lid with old, gritty wires running along the rim and small buttons with faded numbers imprinted on them. She could see the vivid liquid and the microscopic embryo swimming around as the hazardous material penetrated the pores and burned the nonexistent flesh. She could feel the pulsing energy move the liquid to an irregular beat, smashing and splashing up the sides as the pulses pounded against her unborn self. It was too much pain, she removed her hand and the world became calm once more.

“Lita,” her sister's voice was needled in her ears as she turned around.

Vee was looming over a corner with a frigid stance. Her hand was splayed against the surprisingly clean wall. Her shoulders racked with sobs and Lolita rushed to her side.

“I can feel it.” Vee choked out as she kept her head low.
“What is it?” Lolita whispered back, her hand drawing soothing circles on her sister’s back.

“The energy, it is a panic. A mad house. The death, the children's cries before they killed them. I can’t hear their voices, but I hear the gunshots. I hear their knees hit the floor. There is a static in my mind and my hands are numb." Her hand fell from the wall.

Andrevenya fell to her knees and began to weep. She cried and did not care how she looked. She cried for the innocent lives lost in this room. She cried for the lives that never got the chance to breathe or feel the sun on their faces. She cried for the loss of her own life at the hands of her creators who walked proud in this room before she was even truly born.

Lolita continued to rub her sister's back, but gave up with the crying only intensified. She did not feel her comforting hand, probably forgot she was there. So, she left her emotions with Vee and left to collect every file, VHS tape, and audio track she could and shoved it in her bags they had brought. They didn't have much time.

When the work was done and she successfully cleaned the shelves and wiped the computers onto many hard drives; Lolita struck a match.

This roused Andrevenya from her own loathing and mourning. Turning, she wiped the salty tears from her eyes and slowly stood up, eyes never leaving the flame in her sister's emotionless hand. Lolita's eyes attracted to the single ember as it danced for her on the burning stick.

" Lita," she hiccupped. "What are you doing?"

"Sending our creator a message. Grab the bags I have packed there on the table and head for the elevator. Please." The dead voice said as Vee stared at the chocolate hair, unable to see the stone face on the other side. She didn't really want to.

She obeyed and slung two over her shoulder and clutched two more in each hand before going briskly for the shaft and pushing the UP button. It obeyed almost instantly and she stepped halfway inside, waiting for the little girl in the wheelchair who held all the power in the room in which hell was born.

Lolita bent forward, her palm running along the computer screen. It hummed to life as did the others down the row of tables. One right after the other in perfect timing. Abruptly fast, she ripped off the hard drive's protector and yanked at the cords. Clawing till they ripped and live wires sparked their angry embers.

She looked at the match between her fingers and tossed it to the live electricity. The computer popped and crackled like a firecracker. It ran the flame down the wires and the second computer followed suit. Snapping and hissing. The screens turned to loud static before burning out entirely. Grabbing a small travel sized bottle of whiskey from her jacket she had obtained on their plane ride, she smashed it right into the fire. It began to grow. A small little flame aged into a full fire. Roaring till it singed the ceiling. Lolita watched it and sent a spark of heated electrical energy only fueling it more before finally racing to her sister whom waited in the elevator; gawking at the sight before her.

It wasn't the roaring red flames licking hungrily at the table and spare, blank papers and chair cushions that woke Lolita from her second selves hold. It was her sister's strong hand back lashing across her cheekbone as the doors slowly closed in front of them.

"I'm not human; remember that the next time you want to punch my face." Lolita scowled, rubbing the tender skin.

"And neither am I. Try again." Her sister back lashed and sighed leaning at the wall.

"Don't you feel at guilty?"

"I don't have time to feel guilty." Lolita barked back, The gold flickering from the rim of her eyes to the pitch black pupils. "And neither do you!"

"The basement is burning below us! And this place will burn to ashes!"

"And then Luca can't trace back his precious formula and make versions of us he can control from the start." Lolita chuckled, fixing her hair as the elevator doors slid open. The smoke billowed through the floorboards. "I'm glad we are on the same page."

"Same page?! We are completely different libraries!" Vee argued with a shrill cry as they hurried out the front door of the building going up in black smoke behind them.

They made their way over the cobblestone path and around the cliff side, leaving the black smoke in the dust.

“Ok miss, what's our exit plan?” Vee scoffed as she hoisted the sleeping bag back over her shoulder.

“A helper sent by Hollenbeck is gonna meet us at the upcoming intersection to take the bags to the drop off. We go to an abandoned airport just outside of Moscow. It’s unfinished after they built that new one. But a small private plan will be meeting us there to take us and all this information back.” Lolita explained and sighed, hugging the shawl around her face once again.

The rest of the journey was quiet despite the harsh wintering winds slicing against the little exposed skin they had. The drop off person waiting by an old car was none other than Karis with her sly smile as she pushed off and adjusted the blood red scarf around her neck.

“Hey, you two.” She smiled opening the car door as Vee hastily pushed each bag onto the back seats.

“Grant sent you? Isn’t that like, super dangerous on his part?” Lolita asked as she hugged Karis tightly.

The bionic woman only shrugged as she stood up right.

"Nah, it's only brief. I'll be seeing you two on the plane in a few, ok?"

"We aren't driving with you?" Vee questioned as she slammed the door shut.

"Well, no. It would be far too dangerous to have the information and the product in the same little car. Trust me it's easier this way." Karis said rounding the vehicle and climbing into the driver's seat.

The ancient growl of the engine overpowered the sister's rambling questions and Karis was gone down the gravel mixed asphalt road. They groaned in frustration before making their way after the speeding car. It was going to be a long walk.

The snow crunched like dead bones under the wheels and heavy boots as the girls made their way down the trail. The homes faintly lit with candles or weak lamps in their dusty windows. The clouds had thickened and the sun was hidden fully, casting a deep blackish blue aura across the world. The ice covering cars cracked and fell in thick sheets to the dirt road, crashing into splintering shards sliding across the ground.

"We've been walking for hours. I thought the airport wasn't too far?" Vee questioned, her fingers gracing her broken lips. The numb digits only burning the tender flesh.

"I thought so too." Lolita hissed. Her fingers seemingly frozen to the rims of her wheels as she forced herself to push on. "Maybe we didn't make a proper turn?"

"I swear to God if that-" The older woman stopped short and slowly turned herself around.

"Vee? Everything ok?"

"No."

And as if Lolita's blood wasn't already running cold. Two shiny onyx black cars appeared behind the dead towering trees. Their headlights trained on the girls draped in navy shawls. They turned to make a run for their lives, but men as tall as seven feet were waiting at every turn they could possibly make. Some held whips of iron chain link. Others clutched what looked like restraints.

The cars engines roared, taunting them. Lolita turned and focused. She felt the heat radiating from the mechanics and she turned it up. The once chilled blood halting in her veins began to flow faster, faster. Heating to a boiling point. The veins began to glow bright in her arms up to her wrists. A car revved its engine, daring her to continue before speeding straight for the crippled girl. As close as two feet away from plummeting into her body, the car flipped above her head and her eyes caught those of the petrified driver before it crashed against the bodies of his comrades. The flames were enough to warm the girls faces and melt away the thin sheets of ice coating their skin.

“Go ahead, underestimate me again; it will be fun.” Lolita smirked at the last remaining four. Just another set of hooded figures.

They wasted no time and ran full speed at them both. Vee was ready. She threw one clear against a tree a good hundred feet away, before dropping to the ground as a chain whipped across where her head once was. Kicking out her leg, he was down on his side. Her talon like claws drove through his ribs and ripped out the still beating heart. Her senses picked up every energy as it died in the organ. She let it slide off the seven inch nails and roll in the dirt, leaving a trail of crimson.

Her senses did not pick up him within its haze of victory clouding all better judgment.

A fatal mistake.

In a nanosecond, Vee was pinned to her stomach and an iron made collar placed around her neck. It burned like a thousand flames and her scream was ear piercing. The man did not care and bound her wrists to her back in the iron link. The pain was overbearing and her heart was beating so abnormally fast she felt she was going to explode then and there.

"Vee?"

She looked up just in time to watch her sisters breathless and confused expression turn into the same heart exploding agony as the chains wrapped around her throat and yanked her back, out of her chair and landing bone snapping hard onto the dirt. She knew her sister was unconscious. Good thing too. She didn't want to have her see what happened next.

It was a blur even to herself. The torment writhing inside her body as she fought the metals holding her down and the heads of the man holding her down rolling by her feet was enough to make her vomit or pass out, or both. Vee was so lost in the rush of exhilaration, that when she turned back to free her sister; she and the final two were speeding away in the black car. Leaving her alone with the death rotting at her feet.

Chapter 12

"Teper' on stabilen. Prinesite doktora Lyuka."

Now it is stable. Bring Dr. Luca.

The soft hiss of a machine, the words she could not make out were enough to give Lolita a headache despite the blunt trauma she was sure was resting in the back of her skull. Her vision cleared and she found herself in a small concrete room neglecting any color other than slate gray and pearly white, being her blankets. An IV was strung up dripping every so often. She tried to rub away the hair covering her eyes, but her arms fought her. No, not her arms. The straps holding them down. There was no agonizing pain there like when the chain link wrapped around her neck in a cobra grip, but she could feel the stinging sensation prickling her skin. The same feeling the iron gave her. So the straps held her firmly where they wanted her, great.

She stared up at the swinging light over head and huffed angrily. She was caught. Something she promised herself would never happen. She could only pray that Karis had gotten away with her life and the information.

"All my life, I was taught about the angels and the demons."

Lolita snapped her head over to the metal door with bars along the little glass window. It was closed, but an older man leaned against it. Hands sunk into deep pockets. A cold and lifeless smile on thin, withered lips.

"Doctor Luca." She whispered.

"And never before, would I ever imagine my own personal angel, would be one with gold in her eyes, a fire in her heart, and dead bones in her legs." He chuckled quietly to himself even though it was a ringing chorus, bouncing off the concrete walls.

"Yes, child. I'm Mr. Luca."

Even in his elder age, he was quick and nimble on his feet. At her bed side towering over her small and feeble looking body. Admiring his youthful work.

"So… Powerful." He said, running his cold hand along the skin of her hand and stopped at the band of bracelets.

The man mumbled something on the line of *this won't do,* before ripping away the excessive jewelry despite her loud protest. The soft leather, the rubber material of band merch, all useless as it rested on the floor.

There was a quiet that fell over the two. He looked over the numbers embedded under the thin layer of her skin. He smiled and looked back into her eyes.

"I did not know it would work. The numbers being forever marked branded if you will, into your skin. Then again, after all the failures I did not know if you would even survive." He said casually. Like talking to an old friend of his and catching up with remembrance of fond, nostalgic memories.

She stayed quiet, even as he marveled over his work. A classy man with dark and disgusting ideas flowing through his highly intelligent mind.

" There is no greater terror, nor fear, than watching something you have put your life into time and time again, something you love; fall apart at the seams right before your eyes. After Andrevenya's success and the thousands that failed to match her greatness; I felt wronged by the world. Defeated by science and bullied by the masses. But when you remained stabilized, I knew I had my weapons. I had my achievements to give me the glory I rightfully earned from my country. Once I found Andrevenya and had you in my control, nothing could stop me."

Lolita ran her tongue across dry lips, finding her voice and stopping his oversized ego from continuing; having heard enough and a bit over.

"You did not, have and never will, hold power over me or my sister." She promised this man with a fire in her eyes.

Alec Luca bent down, his hand resting on the mattress and it dipped under his weight. She could smell the strong spearmint on his tongue with every word he spoke. The hotness of his air with every time he exhaled.

“Are you sure about that?” It was a dangerous tone and her bones rattled against the muscle with each word she heard. But, she kept a strong face. It was all she had right now.

“Because you are here and your sister will end up in a cell similar to yours. I will bend your minds to how they were meant to be, my dear. Your country does not love you or value the strength you two poses. What have they ever done? Your mother’s boyfriend only appreciated your body and took action on your adopted sister.”

Her body went limp and lips gaped. He smirked at her faltered look.

“Yes, I know *all* about *you*. Did you think you were alone and free all those years? I’ve been there since the day I sent you away from my lab.”

“What happened that day? Why did you abandon everything and leave it all behind?” She asked him. God, she hated how pathetic she sounded. This man was the devil. The all knowing devil and could see right through her eyes, tearing away the veil and armor to see her vulnerable core she could no longer protect with a broken mask.

"The Russian Federation thought it would be in the country's best interest to halt my work. Stop these successful projects. Destroy my children and put my country in danger with the world turning their backs on it." His voice was animalistic as he leaned closer, her body suffocating under the weight.

"You may have escaped your government, but you won't turn me or Vee against ours." She snapped at him. Her gaze staring back at the stones he called eyes.

The man laughed lowly in her face, darting his tongue across his lips before replying to his creation with the fiery personality. He enjoyed her spark. He reveled in her defiance and would love nothing more than to watch it deteriorate into nothing but a hollow wall of what once was a girl. Then, she will be merely a machine to do his bidding.

"You are not going to win this war."

“If I was worried about that, I’d of brought it up when I saw your filthy face walk through the door.”

“You aren’t worried?” He smiled, “ why do I not believe you, sweetheart?”

For a split moment, Lolita confused this heartless man to of been showing her an ounce of compassion. She could not allow her young naive tendency get the best of her.

“Whether you believe in me or not, I will continue to exist.”

His hand was on her mouth before she could utter another comment his way. Her eyes wide in shock and anger burned through them.

“I must say, Lolita. I will enjoy our long time together.” He smiled sweetly down at his experiment before sliding away his strong hand and waltzed to the door.

She thought the eerie man would finally leave her be along with his staff, but a nurse walking in right as her employer left ruined her hopes. She carried a needle filled with a royal blue liquid and she didn't know why her heart was pounding and her nerves were spiking.

“What is that?”

She received no answer. The nurse placed the needle against the tubing and pushed down on the syringe. Lolita’s voice broke out into a panicked plea as she hopelessly watched the liquid flow through the tubing.

“What is that?!”

The liquid hit her veins and the scream that ripped from her vocal cords could be heard through every thick concrete wall of her personal asylum. They shifted from deathly screams to moaning sobs, back to screams of mercy again for hours on end into the late hours of the night. Sleep was dead to the prisoner for the poison refused it. And it was music to Alec’s ears.

“This is place, miss?” The taxi driver mumbled in his poor English.

The harsh ocean wind rolling in from the Okhotsk sea left Andrevenya's skin vacant of any moisture.

"Yes, thank you." She replied, handing him the last of the money she had.

The old car drove off. Back to civilization for this was dead man's land. Not a house or human in sight for endless miles. All except for one.

Silver fog rolled on the black rocks standing firm as monstrous waves crashed against it with no mercy or signs of resting. The vivid contrast of the black ground beneath her was the grass so green but struggled to stay alive. She continued closer to the castle looming on the edge of the world. Dead clouds flowed from its foundation and falling to the breaking water miles below.

As barren and deserted the old castle appeared to be, she knew full well of the lives inside.

Thorns peered over her shoulder as she walked up crumbling stone steps. Decapitated heads made of ancient marble stared lifelessly back at her. Their eyes begging for her to turn around. Run. Get out. Moss decorated the water stained stones building up the high mighty walls. The wolves sculpted out of fine rock above her, outlined by the hazy clouds rolling in, snarled down at the guest as she walked to the front doors taller than any human man.

The only sounds were the whistling winds, peering through the millions of in depth carvings. She heard footsteps approaching the heavy wooden doors and she fled around the wall. A young woman in a clean white uniform stepped out. A cigarette in between her fingers as the other held an old and rusty lighter.

Andrevenya could feel the black ink drip into the whites of her eyes. The brown melt into red. All that was left of the nurse was the old lighter and the blood dripping from bone crunching teeth as Andrevenya slipped inside the castle.

Her claws twitched as her shoes tapped along the cream stone floor. The lobby was beautiful save for the half animal, half human standing in the middle of it under a hundred crystal chandelier. Her teeth relaxed to their natural state and her claws were once again soft manicured nails. Tossing the bloodied scarves aside, she made her way down endless flights of wooden stairs. The world grew darker and her heart froze when she heard the moaning rattle of echoing chains not too far away from the end of the stairs.

Pale green lights flickered on and off as she walked down the hallway. The concrete walls seemed to close in on her. But, that could just be the fear whispering in the back of her mind. Laughter was faint and through the thick walls. Whoever was laughing was no longer living and that alone sent shivers down her spinal column.

She had to find Lolita and get out before she lost her mind in the confines of this insane asylum.

It seemed to be that her prayers were answered. Behind one heavy bolted door with bars on the Plexiglas was a large concrete room. But what was most important was the small body lying in a small rickety bed with blue liquid floating in an IV bag beside her.

The door was easy to open after melting the bolts with extreme heat. In seconds Vee was leaning over the bed and staring down at what once was her sister.

Lolita's skin was an ashy color with the blue and violet veins sticking out against the paper thin flesh. Her eyes sunk back into her skull and were open. They didn't seem to be staring at anything really, but shifted around in fear. All the warmth and happiness that made Lolita the best version of herself was taken away and Andrevenya could only hope she could get it back.

Ripping away the IV from her sister's hand, she pushed the stand away and didn't bother to flinch as it clattered loudly to the floor. With a knife she had obtained from a villager on her travels, she cut away at the restraints holding down her sister. Dipping down, she reached under Lolita's thin legs and around her back to hoist her into her arms and against her chest. The girl was unconscious and weighed no more than a small bag of feathers. It broke her racing heart.

"Lita? I know you can't hear me. But, I'm gonna get you out of here ok?" She whispered into her sister's ear before sprinting out of the godforsaken room.

What once was a quiet and barren hallway was now blaring deep red lights with obnoxious alarms ringing in her ears. Vee kept running, despite the shouting and heavy footfalls behind her getting closer and closer. But when guards aiming chains and whips her way appeared at her only possible exit, she was forced to screech to a halt. She looked behind her, hundreds of doctors and guards were at both ends. They were trapped again.

"0101." Her pulse stopped for a moment as a man in a pristine white coat stepped out from behind the mass. His gaunt features poking her core with a hot poker of fear.

"Luca." She choked out, desperately trying to mask her adrenaline as she lay Lolita against a wall.

"Finally, we meet at long last. I was beginning to think my very first successful monster was trying to hide from me." He held his chest, mocking the pain in his nonexistent heart with a low laugh as he stepped closer towards her.

"And what? You here to finish me off?" She asked him, the fire starting inside.

"No, of course not. Why on God's green earth would I want to kill what is my sure ride to world victory and rightfully earned respect from all of the world's pathetic leaders? No," he stepped closer and she backed away on instinct. The man frightened her but, she could never admit it.

“You and Lolita are staying,” his hand grabbed her wrist.

His fingers shoved away her jewelry and pressed down firm on the numbers lying there. It burned and she winced, tears beginning to rise behind her eyes. Knees going weak.

“Right. Here” He flashed her white teeth as he held her close.

“Yeah, not today buddy.”

The two looked over to see a woman with striking blue and pink hair. Karis smirked before clicking a button on her earring near the top. Small darts shot from the walls and her own body, sending all of the guards, nurses and scientists to the floor in a deep slumber.

Andrevenya took the split second sesh saw the doctor finally beside himself and took her chance. Grabbing his firm shoulder, she flipped him behind her and over her head. The grip on her arm now lost; she ran to Lolita and scooped her back into her safe embrace. Some guards had shifted out from the fallen bodies of their comrades and stood at attention behind their slowly rising leader. Andrevenya stood behind Karis who had her silver gun aimed at the enemies, her heart racing and powers weak from whatever it was Luca had done to her.

“Ok,” she whispered behind Karis. “We have five people a few feet away trying to kill us. What are we going to do?”

“Actually, it’s more like seven or eight.” Her friend replied calmly as they began backing away.

“Oh! I am so sorry I wasn’t specific enough for you!” The older woman snapped, nearly tripping over a comatose body.

“Can you please just calm down, shut up,” she cocked her gun and aimed. “And let me save you?”

Calm down? Calm down?! Vee felt like her intestines were being played with, tossed up and swirled around. Although, that may just be the terrified adrenaline kicking in and doing its part. The gun shot stopped her thoughts as two guards fell back to the concrete, dead. Karis turned and shoved the sisters back all the way to the large winding staircase. Getting the hint, she spun and ran with her sister calm in her grip.

She could hear the power of each bullet soaring. Feel the escaping energy from shocked faces that fell limp and frozen place as their last breath left the body. Karis was on Vee's heels, occasionally spinning back around to end another life with a surgeon's precision. Alec Luca was a lucky man. A man so undeserving of luck, but was always granted it, it looked like. Like luck had a deal that just could never be broken or a terrible consequence would ensue.

If Karis were not there to grab her, Vee would have toppled out the floor to ceiling window pane around the corner. The window leading out to a death drop down into the unforgiving ocean below. Colliding with the rocks, sharpening them till they were sharp spears, skewering anything that dare fall upon them. Vee turned around and the women ducked just as an deranged Luca fired a single bullet Karis's way. His once slicked back hair now wild, disarray with a wolfish look in his stone eyes. The thick pane broke into a million pieces before falling to the water. The man stood upright and adjusted his tie tighter to his neck and exhaled extraneously.

“Enough of the games, sweetheart.” He said breathless and wiped away a guard's blood from his brow carelessly.

“It’s time to come here. So we can get back to work.” The needle of the syringe shone under the rising storms lightning behind them in his hand not occupied by the pistol.

Fear ran across her eyes and stabbed her heart numerous times. She couldn’t go back to being weak, she can’t. She’d rather die.

“Hide your heart my darling. I can see it through your precious eyes.” He began to laugh maniacally.

“And by God, I can’t wait to gouge them out and replace them with something-- better.”

“Ya there’s one problem with that, you gotta catch her first.” Karis’s hard elbow smashed against her arm wrapped around Lolita sent the two falling from the high tower.

Vee didn't hear the tortured scream from her creator. She saw Karis falling above her, preparing for the icy waters heeding hard and fast.

The rocks missed her small body by mere inches as her back hit the water cold as deaths final breath. Holding Lolita close, she kicked her legs till the water surface peeled back and oxygen; cold and ironically dry hit her throat. Karis appeared from the water and swam with impeccable speed, taking the teen into her strong grip.

"Go, I've got her." She shouted over the roaring water and nudged Vee to swim.

They looked back to see Luca watching them swim against the treacherous waters. He disappeared from sight and Vee knew they weren't going to be along in the gulf for long.

The heavy sea would drag Vee under a few times, but she didn't care as long as she came back up to see Karis holding her little sister's head high above the surf. Either it was the hypothermia or fatigue, but her body no longer felt the tingling chill each time a wave struck her. She had long lost sight of the castle for almost a few hours and now saw amidst the heavy mist land across the gulf.

When her bare feet scraped against smooth stones and rough textured rocks, she hoisted herself to stand on feeble legs. Hiding her face, she pushed back the salt water away from her face back to her hairline, before running her fingers through the drenched, nearly black locks and wrung the liquid free at the ends.

The three were greeted by doctors Vee remembered from training with heavy microfiber towels pre heated and needles for hypothermia shots. She could care less about her state; she rushed to the stretcher Karis had laid Lolita on as she was beginning to wake up by coughing up salty water.

"Lita." Her sob escaped her as she hugged the young girl as tight as she could, wrapping them both in her blanket as they sat in the back of the van.

"Miss, please we need to get this IV in her so we can withdraw whatever chemicals Luca may have implanted before there's a relapse." A medic said, gently coaxing her to sit on a bench built into the wall of the now moving van.

She nodded and reluctantly sat still, her eyes never leaving Lolita's as the fluids began pumping into her system. Already the color was returning to her sullen face and her body overall seemed to be improving thanks to whatever it was that was coursing through the IV.

"I'm fine, really." Lita whispered raspy with a weak grin. Her eyes looked around as the medics continued working on her body. Prodding and layering her body in fabric.

"Why are you guys trying to smother me in blankets?" The teen grumbled, pushing them away with her free hand. Vee reached over to hold that hand so the medics could place the blankets back up to her jaw.

"Because you're in shock, hun." She couldn't help but smile at the adorable pout that resulted on her sister's face.

"OK, then that doesn't mean I need blankets. It means I need alcohol." She grunted as she laid back against the pillow.

Vee smiled and rubbed the tender skin of her hand. She could live with her sister being frustrated. She could live with being freezing and ice hanging from the ends of her hair. As long as their hearts were beating and they were together; Vee did not care.

Chapter 13

Three weeks later.

"Hey, Miss Frazier." Jade had slipped under Vee's arm and gone through the door before the woman could even utter a syllable.

"Alright then." The woman grumbled as she let the door shut with a hard flick of her wrist.

Sitting on the couch with the television playing a soap opera, Lolita in the middle, sat with a bohemian patterned and knitted blanket draped across her velvet, silver yoga pants. Her large sweater draped along her olive shoulder, cascading down the other along her bicep. The mug was warm with green tea leaves that swirled around as she pressed it to her lips, but set it back down in her lap upon hearing the unsteady footfalls of her new found friend. Jade had been by her side the morning after she got home. Force feeding her homemade soup, making sure Vee was reminded every ten minutes when Lolita would need her medicine.

"Hey you." Jade smiled, sliding in on the cushions unceremoniously scattered about the floor.

Lolita turned and her now straight, layered hair flowed against her jaw. Her smile skittered across her glossy lips before settling. Fatigue had begun to slip away as the plague of weakness also had started to die inside of her. The color returning to her face and strength in her bones.

"Hey yourself." She whispered for her voice was returning, but agonizingly slow.

"Vee gave you your morning meds right?"

"Yes, of course."

"And the lunch ones are they ready with your spring rolls?"

Lolita couldn't help but chuckle, despite the groaning scratch against the walls of her neck.

"You worry too much, Jade."

The teen slouched with a mere shrug at the statement. Obviously not caring.

"A friend should always be concerned for those they care about. And considering you almost died by this russian man's voodoo or whatever, I thought maybe if I showed some worry about you, I'd be a decent friend." Her serious expression melted away into a tight lipped grin.

"Oh no," The brunette gasped and leaned forward. Her hand vacant from the mug and clutched above her heart.

"Oh god! Lita are you ok?! Should I get Vee?!"

Jade yelped, frantically glancing around the living space, not seeing Vee, whom must have gone off to the bathroom or one of the bedrooms.

"No," Lita winced and choked out, "I think I just felt an emotion."

" I swear to God," Jade hissed with a furious shake of the head and pushed the now laughing Latina back against the couch ever so lightly, still minding the physical pain that did in fact reside. "You about gave me a heart attack!"

Lolita smirked and raised her mug back to her lips, taking a quick sip of the hot tea before leaning forward to set it gently on a coaster.

There was a sing song knock on the door and before either girl could make a sound, Vee yelled *I've got it*, loud enough for the three of them.

They watched Lolita's sister slide along the shiny wood floors in her comfiest socks; nearly sliding into a full split had she not gripped the door handle before the ultimate horror took place.

The door swung open and Karis stood behind it with a starling grin. Her exotic hair flowing freely along the one side of her face. The mesh and futuristic body suits were swapped out for more comfortable and easy-on the-eyes apparel. Her studded jean vest was lazily slung over her shoulder, leaving the Nirvana muscle shirt open for full display and nostalgic glory. The ripped and faded skinny jeans were a nice touch against her black wedge boots. Lolita would always admire the sharp wings coming from her eyes, adding to her sultry and kill a man grin.

“It’s just seems to me the party keeps growing.” Vee said, clearly unimpressed with the day's arrivals and events.

“Wow, what a way to treat the woman who got you out of that mad man’s hands. I saved your life!” The partial bionic woman said cheerily as she glided in the apartment.

Vee scowled and slammed the door shut spinning around to face the annoyingly happy and vibrant younger woman.

“You pushed me off a building!”

“ Hey,” Karis said, walking backward with a shrug. She let the backs of her legs hit the couch and she fell over the back until all Vee could scold were her dangling calves.

“Doing that is giving me all the good karma points I’m ever gonna need.”

She gave a wink to Lolita and Jade who giggled as the older woman stomped over until she was looming over the couch, staring Karis down.

"You're insane, Karis."

Karis scrunched her nose in thought before shaking her head.

"Nah, I prefer creative. Thank you very much."

Seeing Vee had given up and retired to a hanging chair off to the side in the living room, Karis knew she won and swung her legs over to sit upright beside Lita.

"What are you watching?" She asked, leaning to rest her back against the warm leather.

"A soap opera." The girl replied simply, eyes glued to the screen now. She did not notice the confusion on her friend.

"It's all Spanish?"

Lolita leaned forward, took a sip of the tea before nodding and clearing her throat.

"Yeah. It's a telenovela. You've never seen one?"

Karis shook her head no, but her electronic eye, covered by a colored contact; began translating the story in her brain.

“How could you enjoy this?” She asked, utterly baffled. “It has such a dramatic and over the top storyline! It is entirely implausible and totally unrelatable!”

“But, it *is* entertaining, no?” The teen pointed out.

“Well-yeah but that doesn’t make it-”

“It is entertaining, over the top and keeps your attention.” Lolita leaned back and spread her free arms out extravagantly.

“It is a telenovela in a nutshell!”

Vee and Jade both concealed their laughter at the woman's annoyed and exasperated expression. Karis huffed and shoved the girl till she landed on her side against the couch armrest.

“Well, as fun as it is to fight about Spanish actors and the wacky shows they are on, I did come here for a reason.” She said sitting up right.

This caught everyone’s attention. Lolita sat up and hugged the blanket closer to her ribcage.

"What is it?" Vee asked, swinging the hanging lounge chair back and forth slowly.

"Hollenbeck. He has some more tests he would like to run on you two to help with the process."

"And he always sends out his little Hermes to deliver his messages." Lolita finished with an annoyed grunt at the end.

"Exactly, I am the messenger. So don't even think about shooting me." Karis said back with an equal fire.

"Let me guess," Vee huffed, slouching against the faux fur. "He wants us… Today?"

"See, you guys are smart." The woman smiled back at the two frowns that greeted her.

Lolita glanced at her friend who now slumped her shoulders. Clearly upset that their visit was cut so short.

"Sorry," she winced as she moved to get back into her wheelchair, combing her fingers through her hair.

"It's fine. I'll see you guys really soon anyway." Jade said back. Her utmost positivity sparking back to life as she jumped to the balls of her feet.

The teenagers exchanged a brief, but warm hug before Jade was gone. Only the soft clicking sound of the door closing was what was left of her short lived time there.

"You two just gonna wear what you have on or?" Karis asked whilst eyeing the two.

The sisters did the same to one another, saw nothing wrong in the comfortable clothing because they knew they would just be changing into the black mesh body suits, turned back to Karis and nodded in eerie unison.

"Well alright then." Her blue hair bounced with her nod and she opened the door, gesturing for them to leave.

"Shall we?"

The hallway was a sharp pink with matching lights lining all the creases in the walls. Vee hated the color and being surrounded by its cheerful, cupcake aura made her sick. Lolita had already been sent off to her own room. There was no physical training today. No hard and strenuous labor to be done. It was peculiar to say the least.

When the thick door slid open on its own accord before her, the room was small. Much like an exam room in the emergency. Picture frames hung on the pristine walls, but the images were nonexistent. The countertops were clean of any dust or paperwork.

"Have a seat; Dr. Hollenbeck will be with you momentarily." The nurse said in a voice that reminded her of a bell.

She obeyed and swung her legs back and forth, repeating the motion for a while as she sat on the hard bedding. The thin blankets scratched her through the body suit along her thighs, so she shifted away with a wince.

The door slid open and the old man strolled through, nodding her way before searching for the stool on wheels that is hidden under the opening beneath the countertop.

"Sorry for dragging you and your sister back here." He uttered softly to the papers as his pen scribbled along the parchment like a needle on a polygraph.

"Well, you could understand why we were annoyed after you promised us a vacation, as you put it." She replied, crossing one leg over the other.

He capped the pen, a blot of loose ink splattered on the papers edge. Turning and rolling himself to her, he stood fluidly.

"I know. I'm sorry. The scientists who are constantly analyzing your blood, tissue, and all the other data are always demanding more work from you two to analyze. Just in case they find something we were not expecting."

"Has that happened?"

"No, not yet, but we can never be too safe." He said, removing his glasses and cleaning them with the end of his coat.

She nodded. She was once a scientist herself. So, yes she could understand the thrive for more answers and questions all at the same time. The researches within fingertips reach. What data collector in their mind would say no?

"So, what are we here for exactly?" She asked him as he stepped away from her and back to the counter.

He was silent for a few minutes as he reached into high cabinets to retrieve a multitude of items. These being, syringes, cotton pads and rubbing alcohol. A small vial was produced from his deep set pockets. Her curiosity only spiked higher than thought possible.

"Both of you are extremely strong, physically. You have adapted to all of your abilities flawlessly and at a rapid pace, again, physically." He gestured his head and Vee obliged, lying down on the rock of a mattress.

"But, you both seem to allow your emotions to always get the better of you. You get worked up to an extreme and she is on the other extreme end of the scale; lacking any emotion and could easily sway to darker even murderous tendencies if not properly contained and controlled within herself. Now, this." He held up the little glass vial, bottle like container up for her to see.

"This is just to relax your nerves and muscles so restraints won't be needed. Those will do only more harm than good. Your mind however, will be in your full control. Are you alright with this?"

She nodded.

"Of course."

Before the last syllable left her tongue, the needle had already pulled the sedative from the bottle and injected into her bicep. The pain was quick and temporary. It worked almost instantly, for her body was already so relaxed, it was almost paralyzing. Sticky material was stuck to her skin just below the collarbone. Heart pace trackers, blood pressure, and pulse tracking graphs appeared on the monitor beside her hooked on the wall.

"Vee, if you can hear me can you please nod?" He asked, standing over her body and focused on the pupils of her calm eyes.

It took her a minute, but she nodded as her chest rose with a murmur before slowly declining once again. He nodded and turned away for a second. She felt more sticky material rest on her temples and he held them firm till they held their own.

"Now in a few seconds you're going to feel like you are going under anesthetic. When you wake up, you'll be in a realm where it will test your emotions to their limits. When it gets to be too much, I want you to yell as loud as you can; peace. Nod if you understand."

Vee nodded. She felt a warmth trickle from the ends of each individual hair all the way down to her toes. It was soothing, better than any massage. Hollenbeck went pixilated, the whole room was now a mass of pixels and she felt her heart speed up. Everything just felt horribly wrong. Like she was dying or something. She tried to speak, say peace, but her tongue was a wad of dry cotton and she gagged at the revolting feeling. The sharp pixels smeared into damp watercolors. Bright at first, only to fade casually to a solid black. She was all alone.

When she came too, Vee found herself curled up like a cat on a black floor. Her breaths echoed like the choir off walls that weren't there. Shifting onto her hip, she felt softness between her fingers. Looking down, Vee found her body wrapped in fine cloth with a trailing train elegantly laid around her. A gown fit for a Queen. Each finger was decorated in metal talons carved and welded into vinyl patterns with occasional garnets embellished on top. The only light was bright and dull all at the same time.

A clock stood proud before her. The light emitting from behind its frosted glass. The clock stretched so far she was a mouse compared to it. Strong wood beams ran far above her head and attached themselves to the clock, holding it to nothing else but to the arms of the darkness surrounding. The hands taller than herself. Her tall, skinny heels clicked on the floor as she made her way closer to the old fashioned clock. The only thing that jerked her from the view was a man walking from her left. He was a stumpy man. But looked calm and serving. A butler's role, perhaps.

"Welcome back, Miss." This odd man said with a tightened smile. Like screws holding back his emotions.

"Oh," she whispered with her ruby red lips agape in confusion and apology. "I'm sorry you must be mistaken. I've never been here before, trust me."

"Miss," he answered more stern than before. "I never make mistakes."

His hand reached for hers. As soon as she felt the digits wrap around her dainty wrist, they turned to blackest ink. Her shrill cry grew louder as he began to laugh above it when his bod began turning into the liquid.

"Tick tock Miss. Tick. Tock. Miss." His voice faded into her body, becoming ice down her spine.

The jewels gently poked her exposed back with every step she took. Her mind was truly the oddest place she had ever had explored. Before long, a door made itself known to Vee. The clock was clear as day even though she felt she had spent hours on end walking away from it. And there it stood. He could make out every small scratch on its aging face. Her mind no longer was focused on it, however. Her metal talon clicked on the framing before the door opened on its own.

The drawing room was quaint and had a warm invitation. The fire crackled and snapped on the logs nestled in an elegantly simple fireplace off at one end. Overstuffed chairs with hideous green and floral designs on the upholstery. All of that was fine and all, but her eyes were drawn to the small table sitting in the center. When Vee got close enough, she saw the smooth, sculptured chess pieces. They frightened her. There were no knights, pawns or bishops. Each piece both onyx and cream were monsters. Dragons for the Kings, female devils for the Queens and burnt corpses were their tortured pawns.

"Do you wanna play?" The small voice made Vee flinch.

A young girl with messy curls stood across the small table. The wild mess of hair fell to the small of her back. She was thin. Scrawny as a starved dog and she wore a simple pale dress. The fire's warm light casted across her wide doe eyes and the gold burned to life in the amber. Andrevenya had forgotten her childhood appearance and understood why many steered themselves away from her when it came to group home visits.

"Of course." She smiled as they each pulled one of the decorative chairs over to the chess board.

They played the game and their brows mimicked the other being deeply burrowed and creased with concentration.

"Checkmate." Vee smiled softly as she placed the devil queen on her side of the table.

The little girl pouted, her bottom lip glistened against the red flames lighting up the small room. Vee watched her, curious as to why her psyche would bring her youngest self it could remember, back to her in the imaginary flesh.

"Please," she begged, jumping from her seat. "Let's play again!"

Vee tilted her head as she watched her frantically pull her white chess pieces back to her side and sloppily place them back in their positions.

“I don’t know how much longer I’m staying dear.” Vee replied, reaching out for the childs trembling hands.

The little one shook her head, the tangled mess of hair hiding her soft face.

“No! No we have time… Not much time, no time at all! Please.” Her small fingers were cold around Vee’s wrist.

“Before they come for me.”

Her doe eyes were dead with fear.

Before Vee could console the child in her arms, doors flew from the walls and men whose faces she couldn’t make out barreled forward and scooped the child into their arms with her kicking and screaming. For her life seemed to depend on it. Vee couldn’t make out what she was saying in her strangled pleas and hot tears. The fire was a lion. Roaring and masking the cries into soft droplets of water on the sand. The flames licked at the carpet, it now going up in billowing black smoke.

Vee rose to her feet and went to back away, but a blurry man pushed to towards the flame as if she were some sacrifice to subdue the demon until they could get away. Her metal talons dug deep into his shoulder blades. Blood trickled down the metal and onto her skin. It tingled and tickled the flesh beneath but she pushed back. It was when she saw one hold her smallest self above his head over the flame; her heart got the best of her survival. So much so that her mind went blank within the darkness of her dream. When she came too; the room was charred remains of what once was so elegant and wrapped in beauty. The bodies lay in a perfect circle around her. Blackened and the world reeked of burnt flesh. The child was one of them and Vee began to cry. The clock's loud bells drowned her sorrows out.

"Vee? Vee can you hear me?"

When she came too, Vee was greeted by Hollenbeck who stood over her body with a mild worried expression on his otherwise monotone face.

Vee wiped away the tears that had nestled against her cheeks and moved to sit up. The drugs were powerful and stubborn, not ready to let her go just yet, but she fought back and managed to lean her weight on the wall the bed had been pressed against.

“I’m never doing that again.” She muttered with a shake of her head.

“It was too sad. Pointless as well. My emotions still got the best of me!”

Hollenbeck pinched his nose as a squealing passage of air escaped him in mild frustration and maybe even regret. Vee doubted it.

“Where’s Lita? I wanna know how she did.” The woman sighed as she massaged her aching temples while closing her tired eyes from their lack of sleep.

She got no response. So, she peered over at her doctor with the raise of her perfectly sculpted brow.

“Grant. Where’s Lita so I can talk with her?”

He was quiet again and seemed to fumble over words he didn’t even try to form into sounds.

"Grant? How long were we out?"

"Here's a better question. Forgive me for answering a question with another question but," he huffed and sat back down on the stool. "How long do you think?"

Vee shrugged and pursed her lips together, brow scrunching in thought.

"I don't know? Three minutes?"

"It was nearly thirty."

She couldn't stop her jaw from partially dropping at that. Dreams moved so fast when you're the one experiencing them first hand.

"Well, okay. How long was Lita down for?"

Again the silence made a mockery of her and her fury only rose with the fire at the ends of her hair.

"Grant. How long?"

"She hasn't woken up yet."

Chapter 14

Black hairs of the dead dandelions swayed from side to side against the sunset. Lolita blinked a few times and looked away from the shining star. Her head hurt and her wrists ached. The restraints didn't help just like the relaxing medication the nurses had tried first with her overly nervous body. Now, all seemed to be at peace. The grass tickled her arms, the hairs rising to a stand before she sat up with the strength in her middle. She no longer wore her relax around the house attire. Now her form was sculpted out with a form fitted black bodice. The skirt laid elegantly around her bony legs and the sleeves were wrapped around her arms just draping from her tan shoulders.

The crickets chirped loudly by the pond side behind her and she tucked a loose ringlet behind her ear as she looked around. The sun shot out the heavenly streams of light that seemed to cast themselves upon a street like structure. A road, perhaps? She shifted and looked for her wheelchair. It was nowhere in sight and her heart ached. Now how was she going to get anywhere in a mind simulation if she can't even move around the fictional land it had created?

Her arms braced themselves as they dug into the soft earth balling between her fingers. Energy that was foreign and honestly unwelcomed entered through her skin and resting deep inside of her. She didn't like it one bit. It finally subsided and she found herself back in the confines of her wheelchair. The freedom was short lived, but enjoyed.

The road was calm and silent like the dead as she wheeled along the smooth pavement. It was a calm late summer afternoon. Her favorite time of day. Not just yet time for the sun to disappear from her side of the world, but not just high noon. The road melted away from her vision down south. The world acting much like the level of a video game. She only assumed it would be an endless world. But the invisible walls would be there to push her back in. Lolita did not mind it. Wheeling towards the sun, her smile grew to liking the warmth residing there. So calm, so peaceful, too much now the longer she stayed in the trance.

"Lolita." A male voice made her turn.

He was a tall one with a lean physique. She didn't feel threatened by him. She merely wondered why he was in her world. Anyone who knew her knew she wasn't always much of a people person. Why would her deepest psyche create one if that were the truthful case?

"Yes?"

"You're not a hero." His words were so light and heartfelt, she almost thought she had misheard him.

A confused smile appeared instead.

"I'm sorry?"

He walked closer, adjusting his velvet tuxedo jacket firm around his shoulders.

"We wanted you to fight for us. Protect our families. The women, children, defenseless men." The smile withered away. The once vivid and lively rose now a scornful thorn on his wearing face.

"All you do is destroy everything that comes down your path. You have no heart, how could you? Your future will bring nothing but pain, misery, torture for those who never deserved it!" His voice was booming, pounding in her ears, in her soul.

She began to cry as she saw the flowers round her were doing as the strange man had cried; they were dying. Finally, she couldn't take it anymore.

"I was never a human! I never got to really be like you. Like any of them!" The sobs that ripped from her, broke her ribs and crushed her heart in their grasp.

"You can't expect a hero to just fly in with their capes and their strength to save you from every disaster! Some that *you* can control. Man up, woman up, and protect what you can! I'm not going to be this planet's babysitter from all the evils! I am incapable!” She screamed up to his blank stance. It enraged her.

“Then you are a waste of our time.”

She heard the sounds of engines before she saw the mass of black metals flying and driving her way. Her heart began to beat steadily. Quicker--quicker. Did these beings think they could just plow her down and she would not simply wake?

The intense electrical currents flowed from the ends of her hair, the tips of her fingernails, and the pigments in her skin at the cars and planes. In one massive wave, the machinery soared high over her head before crashing and destroying the once beautiful black pavement behind her. Dust and ashes blocked her vision. What was left in its wake, however, was chaos. Blood dripped from the car doors and broken windshields. The closer Lolita got, the stronger the wretched smell of blood and burnt flesh got. Each body she could make out from their charred and nearly unrecognizable state; was a child. None over the age of her own and some young as five years old. Her body froze at the destruction. She did not think of what she had done when it all happened.

Her emotions got ahead of her mind.

Lolita slid her hand over her disgraced face as she let herself mourn. Mourn the loss of life she had so cruelly taken away without a second thought. Mourn her dignity and all she stood for.

Pulling her hand away, bright sterile lights greeted her. The smell of blood and charred remains was replaced by rubbing alcohol and sweet vanilla perfume. The cruel laughter from the stranger was now Vee's worried yet muddled voice. Every rushed word came out rushed and slurred together. In the hazy vision, Lolita could make out the lips going a million miles a second, but never was the best lip reader.

Soon enough, her ears had caught up with the rest of her. The underwater gargling were now becoming solid sentences as she lay on the bed, swaddled like a newborn in preheated blankets.

"She was under far too long! How could you let this happen?" Vee was furious and Lolita did not like it when she was.

"Need I remind you she is still healing from being tortured by a man you had sent us after to retrieve his stupid material?! How could you possibly think it was a good idea? All for the name of science." Vee scoffed in utter disbelief at the man who hung his head like a sniveling coward.

Karis was there too, her hand soothing a warm rag over Lita's forehead, covered ina cold and damp sweat.

"Vee. You need to stop this, right now. She is fine. Hell, we could have kept her under for another hour and a half!" Hollenbeck barked back, suddenly seeming to remember who he was.

"I don't care. You should have kept us together." The older woman sighed as she sat at the foot of her bed, her head hung and tissue now disintegrating in her hot palm.

"Well, you two are free to leave as soon as Lita feels up to it. Which judging by how she's looking at you Vee," Grant whispered over her shoulder, "I bet is quite soon. We will keep in touch that; I can assure you of." And with a nod to the other nurses, they were all out the small door.

The space was calm with the monitor and the breaths falling from the three women was a chorus in the small exam room.

"How do you feel, hun?" Karis asked, not really minding which of them answered her.

"I'm feeling better now. I think just coming back was bit of a trip." Lita laughed as she tried sitting up.

The two ladies were on her in seconds, unraveling the thick fabric that practically mummified her body and helped her keep balance.

"Are you sure?" Vee asked and her sister nodded.

The two hugged tightly and Lolita actually broke into a small set of hardly suppressed giggles. The drugs wearing off would leave her quite cheerful, despite what she may have gone through.

"Ok, well how about we get out of this godforsaken joint and maybe grab some ice cream?" Karis offered, already grabbing Lita's shawl elegantly draped over her wheelchair set off to one corner of the room.

“I’m more on the urge for maybe popcorn.” Lolita replied with her sister nodding.

“Alright, you two can have it your way, just this once since you basically went through some hell.” Karis huffed as she scooped Lita’s legs under the knees and helped her down onto the seat of her wheelchair.

The three smiled and left the horrid room and all of what happened behind the closing door.

Chapter 15

"Vee, that is definitely not true!"

"Oh, of course it is! I read it on Wikipedia!"

"You're arguing this with a girl who has more power in her brain than eight terabytes?

That earned Lita a blank stare in which she rolled her eyes.

"That's really fast and powerful speed and since *when* is Wikipedia a reliable source?"

Vee scrunched her nose in thought before tossing a piece of popcorn onto her tongue with a shrug.

"And this is exactly why you are the human laptop and not me." She said.

"All I want to know is how you managed to, after all we have been through, go onto Wikipedia of all sources and argue with me that there could possibly be any signs of life in the galaxy cosmo redshift seven!" Lita shook her head in disbelief and threw away her empty bag.

She just wished Karis had stuck around to help drag Vee through a long dirty trail of facts about space and the matters of life in other worlds. But, their rainbow haired friend had to run off after remembering the black hole of errands she had to run before the day's end. Besides, the little debate was through and she needed to use the restroom.

“Be right out.” She said to Vee, already slipping her wheels into a small coffee shop beside them in the middle of the bustling city.

Nodding, Vee finally collapsed onto a nearby bench. Her body sore and tired already from the day’s events. And it wasn’t even past two in the afternoon. Social media wasn’t appeasing her either for all the news she scrolled through on her phone was everything she already read or heard about time and time again.

“We never could seem to find new material going on in the world to worry ourselves with, huh Veeve?” Her heart stopped.

Looking up she saw him. Rick smiled down at the woman. Apologetic, sincere, overall glad to see her. The frozen heart was beginning to break.

“Rick.” The name was a ghost on her lips. A haunting spirit she never thought would return. And yet, here he was, leaning against the very bench she sat frozen on.

“I-- I don’t understand. What are you doing all the way here in New York City?” She asked him.

He shrugged and moved to sit beside her. She scooted over as soon as he made the move to do so, allowing him the space he needed. This gave her time to wrap her head around it all.

“You know, I’m not much for the big, cold cities. And New York is all about that.” His laugh could cure diseases, she would swear on it.

“But, I didn’t come here for the delicious pizza or overpriced apartments.” He said and his hand moved to her jaw, caressing there.

She was putty in his hands once again.

“Then what did you come for?” She whispered, her eyes burrowing into his sharp blue pools.

“You,” he said matter-a-fact.

“Why? I thought the reason you left was because of me?”

She watched his calm composure just decay. His expressions now morphed to hurt and realization as he pulled her close.

“No! No no baby, never would I leave because of you!” His hands wove through her hair; they felt natural and belonging there.

“I left because of what those monsters had put in you, Veevee. You don’t understand how much it took for me to leave you and Lita behind that night. I shouldn’t have, but I did and now that I found you both; finally I can help you.” His smile was caring, generous and full of love.

It scared her.

"What do you mean? Help us? I don't get it Rick you're speaking all weird gibberish now." She said, pulling his comforting hands away from her hair and sliding away.

"I called around and found this man who can reverse whoever did this to you and Lita once and for all!" He declared, gripping her hands tight and kissing the soft skin with a burning passion in his eyes and every move he had made.

Rick had found someone? Grant said it was completely impossible to remove the radiation without killing them in the already lethal process.

"Who could have possibly told you that?" She scoffed.

"A man with a whole team. Hard to really remember what he want by? God, what was it?" He chewed his bottom lip, lost in his frantic thought before a light bulb went off in his head.

"Oh yah! Alec, Alec Luca!"

Vee's heart sank to hell. She wasn't given the split chance to reply or even hit him.

“Luca?” The two looked up to see Lolita’s back wheels just leaving the little coffee shop, a look of pure betrayal and hurt on her face that matched Vee’s.

“You can’t trust that man, Rick.” Lolita said, a mother's tone peeking through her warning.

“Lita? No, you don’t understand,” Rick chuckled, glancing between the sisters. “He’s gonna help you. Both of you!”

“He is the one who started all of this!” She exclaimed. Tears were hiding behind her eyes, she shoved them down her throat once again.

In all the craziness happening before her eyes, Vee happened to catch movement out the corner of her eyes. Men in matte black out clothing were making their way across the busy streets. She turned again; Lolita and Rick were distracted thankfully. She moved away from her ex, who finally clicked out of it and focused all of his interests on her. For once, she didn’t want it.

“You betrayed us. Tell them to back off.” She watched his face.

It went through hundreds of phases. Bewilderment to confusion, resting on realization. He shook his head slowly, stepping forward and cupping her gentle face in his all too comforting hands.

"I'm sorry Vee. I-- just can't do that."

"You're going to kill us, if you haven't already." She hissed, blinking away the angry tears in her eyes.

He shook his head as he also began to cry, but only because she wasn't all in on his plan. Something she always did with no hesitation.

"No! I'm saving you don't you get that?! It's messing with your brain baby. It's eating away at your mind. Can't you see it? You aren't yourself."

"No, it's not the chemicals, it's you." Vee snapped, staggering away from the man.

They were getting closer. The panic grew within her belly. It couldn't end like this, they just got home, all ready to move past this hell with these monsters. But, when Vee saw her little sister in Rick's arms, being used as a body shield she knew that anything between him and her was dead.

Andrevenya saw red.

The anger became physical broiling flames that licked up her stomach walls and scratched their metal claws against her skull. Trying to find any way to release its wrath upon the sin.

“Vee, they can help you.” Rick was begging, his strong hands gripped Lolita’s shoulders in a vice grip. Tears may have been in his eyes, but they were crocodile to Andrevenya.

“And what? You’ll believe what any person says to you on the streets?! How dumb can you possibly be, Rick?” She shouted back. Her chest heaved up and down. She felt like she was hyperventilating.

“I really want to help you bebe.” Rick said, his voice dropping in disappointment.

“ You’re gonna be mad at me now, hate me even and say things you don’t mean and that's okay but you are going to thank me! They said I’m allowed to visit you in the hospital whenever we want. Then once you two are better we can go back to our lives! Just like what we wanted.”

Lolita began to cry and Andrevenya couldn’t hear what Rick was whispering into her soft hair. The tears didn’t cease and her head shook rapidly. Lolita’s emotional state left Vee terrified. It meant Lolita was weakened and couldn’t hurt anyone, even if it was a loved one.

Andrevenya felt her pupils grow hot. In a blink, her world was darkened by damp lashes and she felt that tortuous warmth escape her pores. The relief was short lived when she heard the car tires squealing and glass shattering every which way with blood curdling screams.

Opening her eyes, a gasp escaped her before she could stop it. The trees were torches under the sun. Buildings dented inward with cars through their windows in a fiery blaze. The closest bodies were nothing but speckled ashes on the cement. Others lie in the streets and splattered against the brick in horrific graffiti. She couldn't bring herself to turn to her left. Couldn't bear the thought of what she had done.

By God or Lucifer's hand, she turned and tears fell from her eyes. Walking closer, she knelt down and tentatively tapped the spinning wheel now lying on its side. It sizzled against her numb digit and she pushed it away with a scream once she saw Lolita was not there. But, Rick was trapped beneath the searing metals. His once gorgeous face, now a spitting mockery with the soot and thinly sliced flesh. He reminded her of the rare steaks Lolita enjoyed so much. Tender, red, pulsating flesh stark against charcoal black skins.

Rick coughed and wheezed and Vee could hear the broken bones rattle in his chest. She could care less.

“Where is she?” Her voice had dropped an octave and was scratchy from overuse and crying.

Rick only pleaded for mercy as her balled fists gripped his shirt, stuck to his melted skin that sizzled and popped against them. She repeated herself, eyes blazing with fury as she ripped at the stitches of the shirt and her own sanity. Watching his eyes roll to the back of his skull, her own glanced behind him. A blue mazeda sat with the hood bent and crumpled paper in the sturdy stalk of a tree. The window now scattered on the dashboard with a small body lying across it. Lolita's head hung just above the passenger seat, the blood dripping the same pace as the oil.

Andrevenya sobbed as she let Rick hit the concrete while her legs, limp, ran to the car. Lolita was so small lying there. The pretty outfit now stained in hideous red, ashes, and dirt. Her deathly skinny legs hung over onto the hood. Bent at odd angles, one would think they had snapped and broke in millions of places. Not ever knowing they naturally lay deformed, so as Vee placed her shaky hands on the unstable hood, she knew broken leg bones were not on her mile long list of fears.

"Vee, don't touch her!"

Karis's voice boomed against her still ringing ear drums. It was so distorted and wavy; Vee mistook it for her adrenaline bound imagination. When strong arms wrapped around her middle and began to pull her away, she panicked and her body went into a furious chaos of kicking and screaming till her voice went mute. The tears burned hotter than the flames that were caged inside her skin. Her back struck against still warm bark. The wood splintering and scraping against the thin fabric on her back. When the haze faded from water logged eyes, Vee saw Karis staring back at her. The mechanics in the eyes glowing with artificial life The gears turned in the back and no humanity showed, but pain was in her friends other eye. Tears rimming her water line and the black makeup spidered down, cluttering against soft wispy lashes and her bottom lip dared to quiver and break down.

“Don’t touch her.”

Andrevenya made a move and the grip on her shoulders, pinning her to the tree with an iron hand.

“Don’t.”

With a final, broken cry, Vee felt herself hit the concrete, the sliding had done its work and tore up the remains of the shirt she wore. Her eyes took a look around and she saw it all happen as if it was just a nightmare and she was standing behind the one way mirror peering in on the horror.

Men and women dressed in white and baggy suits ran about. Discarding trash aside to pull bodies from wreckage as black smoke mixing with ashy reminisce of once living creatures floated to the blue sky above. Survivors were ushered into white vans with strong, silver bars, running across the windows in the back. Hoses took down the last of her flames that hissed back. Crazed animals, weak but still fighting strong. Enough venom in her to bite at a fighter till he cursed her.

Andrevenya watched as Rick was treated for his severe, most likely third degree, burns. As if he were the victim and not the monster who unleashed her own. The sun beat down on her dark hair, challenging her strength to burn. No matter the way her blood boiled and popped inside her veins, no matter the rushing fluids behind her ears, and no matter the way her eyes twitched every time that man crossed her mind; her heart sunk when she forced herself to look over his wretched and mangled body.

Two men had dipped their strong, white and pristine arms under the ashen body and lifted Lolita out from the rubble. Glass fell from her chest with clogged, dry blood. Smoke rolled under her body. The image of a sacrifice that did not need to be made.

It's all your fault.

You're the reason she's probably dead.

It is all your fault.

You were built to destroy everything you have ever loved.

It's all your fault.

" Vee, it's time to go." Karis held her friend whose hands hid her face.

The blood that was not her own smeared against her cheeks. Karis knelt down and with an arm across her friend's shoulders, hoisted the woman to her feet and shielded her face from the hell just a few feet away. Helping Vee into the van, Karis swept across the horrendous sight. So many brains will have to be cleaned from it all. So much wrath will rain down with the Big Man himself and she knew this was going to ruin Hollenbeck's day. Sitting down, her eyes fell to Vee.

She had seen a lot in her own young life. So many cowards and pitiful people. Never had she seen a person, her friend no less; look so pathetic and broken down. She could understand why. As the crime scene grew smaller and smaller in the window, her heart sank a little more.

"This is going to change everything."

Epilogue

"A coma."

Her voice was strained with a host of emotions, yet dead to the words that formed there.

The sun was no longer high in the sky, but just high enough to be bright and blinding to the eye while Vee sat nervously tapping her foot to the air on the private jet. Grant was staring back at her across the mahogany table. Blank stares of contemplation met one lost to the universe, not caring what happened in its hand. The sun was caught by her eyes and tied down with the gold reflects within.

Grant released a soft grunt before leaning his back against the soft cushions. Shaky, gnarled hands removed his glasses and wiped the lenses on the soft of his shirt. Vee didn't understand why, they were clean as could be.

"A blow to the head upon hitting two people and then going through a car window can cause significant damage to the brain no matter how impressive it may be. We are lucky though. Her body's a quick healer, mentally. The mind constantly working to update and fix itself like technology is, well, miraculous and we should thank our stars she is who she is or else Lolita would be on life support for only a few days before going entirely brain dead." He said.

"So I should be happy? Happy that I put my sisters life at half a risk than what it could have been?" She snapped and reminded herself to thank the nurses for the sedative they provided her before boarding the plane. Or else a repeat of what happened an hour ago would have occurred in the very spot she sat.

"Vee, I didn't say that. Now look, we had to get everyone out of the city who knew you. Danny and Jade are on the next flight out to meet us." Hollenbeck said, irritated and just tired at that point, the creases in his face deepening.

"Meet us where?" She asked.

There was a silence again and if silence were a human being or some living creature that could feel pain; she would make sure it never forgot it. He shifted again, his body gesturing to her window no longer lit up with the hot sun as the plane tilted in the sky.

Vee peered through and saw sand. Dunes rising high on the earth and trickling down into endless seas of the same tans and beige. A wasteland, void of any life. All except for the stark black top paved in giant formations on top of the grainy earth. Cacti dotted the planes with speckled greens. Multiple little buildings of gray slate were plotted along the pavement as well. But no sign of human life. A barren site is what it looked to be.

Her eyes turned and met the man. Seriousness engulfed him and her heart began beating eighty miles a second. Leaning back in her seat, she turned till she caught a glimpse of Lolita. Small and frail in the makeshift hospital bed. The sun casting a heavenly light upon her body clothed in tightly wound bandages from her breasts and down to her thighs in a twisted sort of dress. The angelic sheets tucked against the gauze and bandages kept her modest to those on the plane. Loose curls framing her face. The embodiment of youth and the future. Hollenbeck's soft grunt pried her away from the girl and back to his attention.

"Welcome to Area 51."

TO BE CONTINUED

ABOUT THE AUTHOR

In a rundown shed during a horrible Siberian blizzard, a baby was born and left in an orphanage in Russia. Kelsey Minick was left a paraplegic due to child abuse with her foster family.

Now, being one in a current family of 10, inspiration was everywhere. She started out with ballet at five getting the role as Clara's little sister in the Nutcracker Then, in 2009, had starred the lead role in the personal film: More Than Chance.

The small film opened a world of opportunities and new passions and goals to be filled. Many of those goals were accomplished and new ones were created through being in 10 plays and 2 films.

"Just because you have a disability, doesn't mean you can't follow your dreams"